The Girl Who Ate ✶ ✶ Chicken Feet ✶

by Sandy Richardson

Dial Books for Young Readers *New York*

Published by Dial Books for Young Readers
A member of Penguin Putnam Inc.
375 Hudson Street
New York, New York 10014

Typography by Amelia Lau Carling
Printed in the U.S.A. on acid-free paper
First Edition
1 3 5 7 9 10 8 6 4 2

Library of Congress Cataloging in Publication Data
Richardson, Sandy.
The girl who ate chicken feet/by Sandy Richardson.
p. cm.
Summary: As she grows up in Midville, South Carolina,
in the 1960's, Sissy's life is especially shaped by her
relationships with her grandparents, her mother, her bossy cousin,
and the black woman who cooks for her family.
ISBN 0-8037-2254-0
[1. Family life—South Carolina—Fiction.
2. South Carolina—Fiction.] I. Title.
PZ7.R398115Gi 1998 [Fic]—DC21 97-9687 CIP AC

This book is dedicated to
★ Mooney and My Two Muses ★

A very special "Thank you" to
Toby Sherry
Dianne Johnson-Feelings
Victoria Wells

and much love and appreciation to
Martha, Jayne, Michelle, Jack, Kwame, Donna,
Lynn, Niani, and
MOST ESPECIALLY, to my family.

I love y'all!

★
Contents

The Gypsies Who Stole My Name

"Hot-doggit! I'm goin' to cook that goose yet!" Big Daddy slammed the back door and threw his hat on the table. It was the second time in three days that Queenie had nipped his leg, and my granddaddy had just about had enough of her.

"Now, Bill," Granny said, "you know you aren't goin' to cook her. You'd have to catch her first, and she's too smart for that." Granny and Elease, our cook, laughed together in the kitchen. Big Daddy mumbled something under his breath and walked on down the hall.

Queenie showed up in Granny's backyard not too long after my daddy got his new job. Big Daddy says Daddy brought her here to guard us since he was traveling so much, but that's just not true. We don't need a guard goose. Granny takes care of my sisters and my baby brother while Mama's at work, and I'm ten years old, so I don't need much looking after. Queenie just invited herself to move in with all of us. She nested under the porch steps, way back where we can't reach her, and every time a man comes into the yard, she bites him. She comes charging out from underneath the house, squawking and honking with her long neck stretched out flat and straight in front of her, her orange bill open and ready to take a chunk out of the back of a leg. Everybody in town knows about her—even the preacher asks how our guard goose is doing.

But Queenie's not the only strange thing in Midville, South Carolina, these days. It must have something to do with those changing times that the news people say 1960 will bring, and Queenie could be one of those omens Elease talks about all the time. Granny doesn't think much of Elease's omens, but Elease knows about things most white folk can't even dream, and I believe her when she tells me about them. Elease has never lied to me one time, and I've known her all my life.

The strangest thing of all is that everybody in Midville is different these days. All the grown-ups in town seem mad about something, and some of them won't even speak to us anymore. I heard Granny and Big Daddy talking about it one day. It has to do with the colored people down in Mississippi and Alabama. But when I asked Granny about it, she said, "These are just confusin' times, child. Everybody's all up-stirred. Best just do as you're told and don't get into any trouble. It's not your worry."

Granny's right about that. Besides, I have my own worries to think about, and my biggest ones are my baby brother, Carson junior, and the hex the Gypsies put on him. Big Daddy and Granny make over him like he's the same as that son in the Bible who went away and then came back and was treated so special by his daddy. And it's not like he just got here or anything. Carson junior's a year old, but they aren't getting tired of him yet. They still go on about him being a boy, and for me, nothing's been the same since he came.

Even Elease makes over Carson. Elease has been with my family forever, and she took extra good care of me because I was her special girl she said. She'd cook all my favorite foods, especially her homemade applesauce, but now she makes it for Carson junior. She spoons it up to his mouth and says, "He's just the onliest boy baby we's gots 'round heah," and then she smiles with all her teeth, which she hardly ever does.

I don't know how my sisters, 'Becca and Arlene, feel about it; I guess they're too young to notice much, but for me it's hard not to feel mad. And then when I feel mad, I start feeling guilty, because I know I'm supposed to love my baby brother. But trying to prove it only made things worse—on top of Carson junior getting hexed, those Gypsies stole my name.

My best friend, Polly, is the only other person in the world who knows about the hex, and I sure can't tell the others because it's all my fault their precious baby boy is going to grow up with a spell on him. Polly thinks maybe he'll grow out of it, but even if he does, it looks like I'm never going to get my real name back, because now everybody calls me Sissy, even Polly.

First of all, I wasn't supposed to cross Highway 15, the road that goes all the way to Florida. Big Daddy says that around Christmastime every Yankee in the world rides Highway 15 south to Miami Beach.

"They just whiz by in those big shiny cars and don't care nothin' about the speed limits. All they think about is that sun and warm weather waitin' down in Florida," he fusses. "Y'all stay away from that highway, ya heah?"

And we always had stayed away from it. But when I saw the Gypsies coming into town, everything changed. I guess things get pretty crowded down in Florida, because every Christmas when the Yankees go south, those Gypsies come north to South Carolina, and this year they came to Midville.

A big group of them came three weeks before Christmas. Polly and I were sitting on the steps outside the post office that Saturday, and we just couldn't believe what we saw. The cover on the first wagon was an old green tent with faded-out black letters that spelled U.S. Army on it. The tent part swung to one side every time the horses' hooves went *clip,* and then it leaned the other way when the horses went *clop.*

"Do you think it will tip over?" Polly asked me as we watched the wagon coming closer. I didn't answer her because that *clip-clop* sound got into my feet and made me want to get up and dance. The string of little silver bells that hung over the man's shoulder tinkled in time with the horses, and I was thinking hard about keeping time with the music the wagon made.

The man guiding the horses sat high up on a board seat with a big floppy hat hiding his face. People around here say Gypsies are dirty, but the man didn't look dirty to me. His hat was pulled down over his eyes, so I couldn't really see his face, but the arms that stuck out from his shirt sleeves just looked brown—not a dirty kind of brown, just brown like he had been in the summer sun for too long. And his shirt was about as white as white could be. Somebody had worked hard to get it that white.

The man tipped his hat at Polly and me when he rode by, and we watched the back end of the wagon waddling back and forth just like the front end had.

Then the second wagon came by, pulled by two black horses, and even though I didn't know it then, that wagon brought all my troubles with it. The sides of this one were covered in red cloth, and strings of silver bells hung all around, like the silver garland on our Christmas tree. The bells jingle-jangled as the horses passed in front of us, and Polly and I held our breaths because across that red cloth was spelled out "Madame Margo—Fortune-Teller" in giant gold letters.

I jumped up from the curb and ran over to the side of the wagon, skipping alongside of it to the end of the block, with Polly chasing behind me. We stood on the corner by the dead crossing light as the wagon tinkled its way across Highway 15 and turned behind Mr. Soothe's red-dot store onto the dirt road that led back into the woods.

"Did you see that, Polly?" I asked. My words came out chopped-up and fast.

"Yeah," she said.

All that night I thought about those Gypsies, especially about Madame Margo and the story I had heard Elease telling Granny about fortune-tellers. Elease had said how, right after she was married, she went to see a Gypsy fortune-teller who could do spells and things on people. Elease thought maybe a spell might help solve her troubles with her husband, Samuel, and his other women friends. That fortune-teller stuffed a little bag full of something to give to Samuel that was sure to straighten him out good. It was a magic potion, and she told Elease not to open the bag, just to tell Samuel where it came from and hand it over to him saying, "If ya don' quit ya tomfoolery, dis is what's gwine to 'appen to ya!"

Elease told Granny that she did just like the fortune-teller told her.

"I wanted to open de bag, Miz 'Melia," she said, "but I held back and just felt it all over with my fingers on de way home.

"It was all soft and squishy feeling. I smelt of it, and pheww! what an awful smell it was! When I gots home I found Samuel lyin' in bed, and I jerked dose covers from off him and shoved dat little bag right under his nose. Then, I said jus' what the fortune-teller tol' me to say. Samuel, he sat straight up when he heard her name, an' he didn't wanna take dat little bag, so I jus' tossed it over on top of him.

"Samuel, he jumped up quick, grabbed dat bag, an' raced out to de field. I saw him standin' out dere feelin' it all over. An' real careful like, he took out his pocketknife an' slit de bag open. Whatever was in dere plopped to de ground, an' Samuel, he started to jump up an' down, stompin' all over de thing. He come get de shovel, dug a deep hole, an' buried dat bag an' all. I never did find out what was in it, but whatever it was sho'ly worked on him all right. Samuel been jus' good as gold ever since."

'Course, Elease and Granny don't know I heard that story, but ever since then I had been hoping to get to see a fortune-teller myself. So when Madame Margo came into town, I thought she was just what I needed to make things like they used to be. There were some people in my family that needed to be straightened out good, and so after I saw Madame Margo's wagon, I started making plans.

Mama and Granny were taking 'Becca and Arlene into Huntstown the next Saturday to see my aunt Boo and cousin Delores, and for once they weren't making me go along. So Saturday seemed to be the perfect time for me to visit the Gypsies. Polly and I talked it over, and we planned all week about how to see that fortune-teller without getting caught. But then Mama almost ruined the whole idea.

"Amy Claire, while the girls and I are in Huntstown, Elease has a lot to do around the house, so you're goin' to have to help her out by watchin' Carson junior."

"But, Mama, Polly and I have stuff we want to do."

"Well, you'll just have to put it off. It's time you learned some responsibility. Elease won't be around forever to do it all for you."

I wondered what she meant by that. Maybe Elease is going away somewhere like those colored people in Mississippi and Alabama. But Elease never says anything about all of that, and I didn't think about it too long. The Gypsies were more important. I cried and whined, but then Polly came up with the idea to take Carson junior with us.

"We can take him in the wagon," she said.

So that's just what we did. I waved good-bye to Mama and Granny, and I told Elease I was taking Carson junior to play with Polly's little brother. Polly met me behind the post office, and we pulled the wagon over the dirt path that led to the pine trees that grew along Highway 15. When we were sure no one was watching down our way, we took a running start across the road. Carson junior usually liked riding in the wagon, but we started off so fast, he tipped backward, and then the wagon wheel hit a rock in the middle of the road, and the wheel twisted and locked up, and Carson junior went flying toward the front, almost falling headfirst onto the pavement. I pushed backward on the wagon handle trying to get the wheel unlocked, but it wouldn't turn, so Polly lifted the back end while I picked up the front, and we carried Carson junior and the wagon to the other side of the road. It was a wobbly ride for him, but he didn't cry, just smiled and drooled, like usual, and Polly and I rested a minute before we moved on. Crossing that big road all by ourselves for the first time was tiring.

When we had rested, Polly helped me twist the wagon wheel back in place, and we hurried on through the woods on the other side of Highway 15. There wasn't any path on this side, and the pine needles were thick like a rug, so the wagon gave us even more trouble as we twisted our way through the trees. But finally we came up behind Mr. Soothe's store and turned to follow the dirt road back to where the Gypsies were camped.

We smelled them before we saw them. A big iron pot was bubbling over a fire in the center of the camp where two women knelt on the ground cutting up onions and carrots to toss into the pot. The horses were tied to an oak tree, and just as we reached it, a big white dog, followed by a pack of smaller black and brown ones, rushed up to us. The white dog's hair stood up all along his backbone, and the other dogs growled until the women by the fire turned to shoo them away. Then one of the women walked over to us. She looked like she could be the witch in the Hansel and Gretel story—short, skinny, and ugly.

"Well, now, who have we here?" She circled around behind us and stopped to kneel in front of Carson junior.

"Hello, my pretty boy," she smiled.

I couldn't help wondering why everybody was so crazy about little boys, but I didn't say a word out loud.

"Come on in. Come on in," the Gypsy witch said

as she took the wagon handle from my hand and pulled Carson junior up close to the fire. Polly and I stumbled along behind them.

Then the other woman stood up and came over, and Carson junior just smiled and drooled while they talked baby talk to him. The dogs slunk back under one of the wagons, and Polly and I stood stiff legged, waiting for somebody to notice us.

"What brings us these fine visitors, do you think, Margo?" the Gypsy witch asked the other one, and they turned together to stare hard at us. "Young ones aren't they, hummmm? Tell me, girls, what brings you to our camp all alone and with such a pretty baby? Do you want to sell him, maybe?"

Then they both laughed out loud. Some of the Gypsies heard the laughing and came over to stand around us too, and right then I remembered Elease saying how Gypsies used to steal babies. I swallowed hard. Granny and Elease would kill me for sure if those Gypsies took Carson junior. And Big Daddy would probably do something even worse than that. He said Carson junior was the son he had never had.

But before I could think of anything to say, Polly sputtered out, "No, m'am, she's not sellin' him. She's just tendin' to him."

"Yes, m'am, that's right. I'm just tendin' to

him," I repeated. "I tend to him all the time. My mama's teachin' me responsibility, and he's it—my responsibility, I mean. I wouldn't ever sell him, no, m'am. I couldn't. And please, m'am, don't steal him. My mama'd kill me for sure." My words tumbled out all over each other.

"Responsibility, hummmm? Well, now, that's a fine thing to be learning, for sure. And, of course, I wouldn't want you to be killed if I took him, so if you're not selling him, why then are you here?" The Gypsy witch laughed in a squeaky high voice and patted Carson junior's curls.

"I c-c-came to get my fortune," I stuttered.

"To get your fortune?" the men laughed.

"I mean, I came to get my fortune told and to get a potion to straighten out some people, please, m'am." Then I told her all about Elease and Samuel, but I didn't get the story exactly like it happened because the words rushed out before I could put them together right.

"And you want a potion to straighten out some people in your own life? Tell me about it, little one."

I tried to slow down my words, but by then Polly was kicking the sand with her shoes, and I knew she wanted to get out of there. I wasn't feeling too good about being there either, so I hurried through the story about how my whole family was crazy over Carson junior and didn't pay any attention to me anymore.

The woman smiled a secret kind of smile and when I saw how she looked at Carson and patted his head, my stomach rolled over. I said a quick prayer up to God Our Father to please not let them steal him.

"Fortunes, hummmm? Well, now, do you have any money, honey?" The crowd laughed again.

"Money?" I asked and looked over at Polly, but she shook her head.

"Uh, no, m'am. We didn't think it cost money."

"Well, now. Let's see. Perhaps we could make a trade. Say, your fortune told for . . . ahhh, yes, this pretty baby boy here?"

I swallowed again; Polly hiccuped, and the crowd laughed harder. But then Madame Margo held up her hand and all the laughing stopped. She stood in front of me, frowning at the others. She took her long, red fingernail and started at the spot between my eyes and followed my nose down to the tip, where she tapped it three times.

"Enough!" she commanded. "Come, girls, come." She motioned for us to follow her to the red wagon with the gold letters.

A breeze jangled the strings of silver bells and a cold chill crawled up my back. Polly rubbed her neck, and I knew the hairs there were standing straight up.

"Come, girls," Madame Margo said again.

I picked up Carson junior, and Polly and I followed her into the dark quiet of the wagon. The other Gypsy woman followed us inside.

Beads and bells hung everywhere, sparkling in the light from a lantern. An old couch, covered all over with bright green and red pillows, stretched across the far end of the wagon. Madame Margo squeezed between a chair and a small table and plopped herself down in the middle of the pile of pillows. The witch woman sat on the floor, near us.

"Now, girls, let's see, what kind of potion do you need?"

I looked over at Polly, thinking she would go first, but she wouldn't look at me. I stared at her, waiting, while Carson junior tugged at a string of beads that hung over my shoulder.

"No," I whispered to him, afraid to speak out in the dark of the wagon. The Gypsies sat staring at us while the quiet grew longer. I cleared my throat to talk, but Carson junior yanked at the string again, sending the silver beads pinging onto the little table and all over the floor.

"Oh, no, Carson junior! Look what you did!" My voice sounded loud and hard in the wagon. Madame Margo looked closely at me.

"There'll be trouble to pay for sure," the Gypsy witch whined. "Those are magic beads. To break the string could cause terrible things to happen, you know." She looked from us over to Madame Margo, who smiled a closed-up smile at her friend and then turned her back to us to fluff a pillow.

When she looked up, her eyes were big and black. The quiet of the wagon grew loud again, and I knew right away that I shouldn't have come. Polly squirmed beside me, and Carson junior wet through his diaper onto my pants.

"Give me your hand," Madame Margo ordered. She held my palm close to the lantern, and with that same red fingernail she followed the line that began at my wrist and curved up between my thumb and first finger.

"Hummmm," she muttered as she stared at my palm. I bent over to have a closer look too, but I couldn't see anything there except a blister that was starting to rise because I had pulled so hard to get the wagon through the woods.

"You do indeed need help, little one, a spell per-haps," Madame Margo began. "But there will be a price."

"But we don't have any money," I told her again.

"Ah, such a life—so full of strife," crooned the old witch. I was getting tired of her silly rhymes.

"But I want things to be the way they used to be," I said, trying to hide the tears that were filling up my eyes.

"Very well, then. Just leave the baby boy with us, and your problems will be solved. He will be out of the way, and you will have your proper place in the family again." I wished the ugly Gypsy would leave.

Polly hiccuped again, and my stomach rolled over on itself.

"But I c-c-can't leave him, Miss Madame Margo."

"You said yourself that he is the cause of all of your troubles."

"Uh, y-yes, m'am, I know, but I still c-can't leave him."

"Well, then, I don't know what we can do for you," she snapped back. "You have no money and nothing to trade. It is such a shame! And we must not forget the beads. You must pay for the beads. Surely you have something to trade."

The Gypsy witch smiled at Carson junior and reached out her hands to take him from me.

I held on to him as tight as I could, but Carson junior reached toward her. She sat him on her lap, not seeming to care about his wet pants, and hummed a strange tune in his ear. Carson junior patted his little hands together. He didn't know that he was being stolen. His eyes shined bright blue and happy while he laughed at the music the woman made.

"Please, m'am, please. Don't let her take my baby brother," I begged Madame Margo. Polly sat more still than a statue, and I wasn't even sure she was still breathing.

The fortune-teller reached up to wipe at my tears. "There, there, child. We'll think of something else. Let's see. What is your name, little one?"

"A-Amy Claire. My name is Amy Claire."

"Well, Amy Claire. I think I have the answer to your troubles."

"You do?" I asked, wiping my nose on my sleeve.

"Yes, yes, I think I do. Now, the problem is that you are unhappy with your life. . . ."

"And she owes us for the beads, don't forget," the other Gypsy added.

"Yes, of course, the beads. Well . . . what do you say . . . we will give you what you want. Let me think a moment." Madame Margo gazed into the space above my head. "Yes, I think this might do. In exchange for a magic spell, you must bring us a fine Christmas dinner. Do you think you can do this?"

I didn't see how I could, but I nodded yes anyway.

"But she might not keep the bargain, Margo. We must take something of hers before we let her go." The ugly Gypsy slid her eyes toward me.

"Yes, yes, we shall," Madame Margo agreed. "I think I know just the thing. Amy Claire, you must leave me your name until you bring the Christmas dinner. You shall have your wish—things will be better, you'll see."

"But if you break your word . . ." the Gypsy witch added, her voice fading away as she patted Carson junior on the cheek.

It was getting late. Granny and Mama would be home soon, and I wanted to be there too, but after all Polly and I had been through to get to the fortune-teller, I didn't want to leave without that spell. I didn't let myself think about what would happen if I couldn't get the dinner. The Gypsies could have my name. That was silly anyway. Nobody could take your name.

"Is it a bargain, then, Amy Claire? I shall keep your name, and you will bring me a fine Christmas dinner," Madame Margo nodded.

"Yes, m'am, I'll do it," I promised.

"Or else," the witch whispered softly.

Madame Margo smiled, then bent to mumble some strange-sounding words over my palm. I had my spell at last!

"Now, we must give you a new name to use until you complete the bargain, heh?" She took Carson junior from the other Gypsy. "What shall we call your big sister, baby boy?"

"He can't talk, m'am," I said, reaching over to take him from her lap.

"Why, of course he can talk, can't you, precious one?" Madame Margo pushed my hands away. "Talk to me, baby boy. What shall we call your big sister, hummmm?"

The red fingernails tickled Carson junior's chin, and the fortune-teller mumbled more words I couldn't understand. She's putting a spell on him, I thought, but he didn't seem to mind. He smiled and then turned to point at me.

"Thithy, Thithy," he gurgled.

The Gypsies laughed out loud while Polly and I stared at Carson junior.

"Sissy it shall be then!" Madame Margo lifted Carson junior high in the air and then handed him gently to me.

"I'll keep your other name in this pouch, Sissy." She dug into the side of her long dress, pulling a small black pouch from the pocket.

"Go now," she said, and we left the Gypsy camp a lot faster than we had come. The wind was blowing harder, and the air was cooler as we hurried toward home with Polly pulling the wagon while I carried Carson junior in my arms.

It was later that same day when Granny heard us on the porch. "Thithy, Thithy," Carson junior said over and over again, pointing at me.

"The precious can talk now, yes he can," Granny crooned. She told the whole family, and they thought I had taught him to say it. Carson junior and I got a lot of attention those next few days. Granny even told the neighbors, and the preacher announced it in church on Sunday, so before long everyone was calling me "Sissy."

Carson junior talked a lot after that. It was like all the words that had been pushed at him were coming out at one time. I stayed close by just in case he said the wrong ones; Polly and I worried that he might say "Gypsies."

*   *   *

But there wasn't too much time to worry. Fixing for Christmas is always the best time at Granny's house, especially when Tyrus comes up from the other farm to help out. Tyrus is Big Daddy's right-hand man, and everybody loves having him around. Nobody is better than Tyrus at hunting, fishing, cooking, or just joking around.

He came to Midville the day before Christmas, so that he and Big Daddy could fire up the barbecue pit early that morning. They cleaned and dressed the pig and spread it out over the hot coals to cook until Christmas morning.

Big Daddy kept me busy carrying things between the kitchen and the pit, because Queenie was on guard at the back porch and wouldn't let either of the men get to the house. I toted and hauled Elease's secret sauce all afternoon while Big Daddy and Tyrus fed the fire and drank up Big Daddy's Christmas whiskey. By late afternoon the whole town could smell our Christmas dinner, and I was proud to say that I had helped.

Then Polly came over, and when Big Daddy and Tyrus fell asleep in the sun, Granny called us into the house.

"Sissy, you and Polly walk down to the post office and see if my package from the Sears and Roebuck has come in," she said.

I was glad to get a rest from the toting, and we started off in a hurry, but before we could check on Granny's package, a voice sneaked up behind us on the sidewalk, and we froze right there at the door of the building.

"Ah, Sissy and her friend. It is almost Christmas, and I have been thinking of you all the day long." The Gypsy witch moved in front of us to block our way.

"And how is your baby brother today? You haven't forgotten our bargain, now have you?"

"Uh, no, m'am, we didn't forget," I said as Polly hiccuped beside me.

"Good, good. We shall expect you soon. It smells as though someone's dinner is almost ready, hummmm?" The Gypsy smiled her widest crooked smile while she sniffed the air and swished her skirt against our legs when she turned to leave.

"What am I goin' to do, Polly?"

Polly said she didn't know, and the walk home was long and quiet.

When we reached Granny's house, Big Daddy was standing just beyond the back steps, staring at

Queenie's stretched-out neck and beak. "Sissy, come here, girl," he shouted. "Take this bowl back to Elease and bring me some more sauce." His arm stretched to the side so that I had to walk between him and Queenie to get it. Polly giggled behind me.

"Cussed goose. I'm gonna get you yet," Big Daddy mumbled as he walked back to the pit.

Queenie waddled back to her place under the steps, and I stooped down to look into the dark where she hid.

"What are you doin', Sissy?" Polly knelt in the dirt beside me.

"Do you know anythin' about cookin' a goose, Polly?"

"Huh?—Sissy, you're not thinkin' about cookin' Queenie are you?"

"Well, what else can I do? Those Gypsies aren't foolin' with me, Polly!"

"All they've got is your silly old name. Don't worry about it. Just keep the new one. It's easier to say anyway."

"It's not just my name, Polly. If I don't keep the bargain, they're gonna take Carson junior. I can tell by the way that mean Gypsy witch talked today. Didn't you hear her? She means to steal him, I know she does, and then I'm gonna be killed by my whole family!"

"Well, you can't cook Queenie. Even if you could catch her, we don't know how to cook a goose."

I knew Polly was right. I had to think of something else, but that didn't seem like it was going to happen, because Granny kept me so busy, I didn't have time to think too hard. Polly had gone home when Granny sent me back out to the fire pit.

"Big Daddy, Granny says for you to keep this tray out here, and then you can bring the whole pig in on it first thing tomorrow mornin'."

Big Daddy grunted a sleepy answer and tilted his chair back against the tree trunk, pulling his hat down over his eyes again. Tyrus snored in the rocker beside him.

Streams of smoke floated up into the cool night air, and the fire hissed as drippings from the pig fell down into it. The smell was too good to stand. The pigskin curled, all crispy brown, but when I reached over to pull a piece away, the whole left ham pulled loose and almost fell off the grill. That's when the idea came to me.

It was late, but I ran to Polly's house anyway. She didn't much want to help me, but she gave in after

I promised to let her ride my new Christmas bike I had found hidden in the toolshed. I had to loan it to her for a week, though.

We waited until Big Daddy and Tyrus left to get another load of wood for the fire. Then Polly helped me fit the pan up close to the open edge of the pit so that the hot meat would slide right off the grill and down into it. The loose ham went in first with a loud *clank!*

"Shhhh—somebody'll hear us, Polly." She stuck out her tongue at me.

The other ham fell as easy as the first, and we dragged the shoulders down the wire to the edge to plop them in too.

"What about the ribs?" Polly asked. "They're the best part."

We pulled at the skin underneath them, but it was thick and wouldn't come loose.

"We'll make do with what we have," I whispered to Polly. I hoped that this would be enough to feed all of those Gypsies.

"We better leave somethin' for Big Daddy and Tyrus," I said. "Maybe they won't miss the hams."

Polly took one handle of the big tray while I lifted the other. The hams were heavy, and the metal tray was almost as long as we were tall, so our steps were slow and careful. We lugged that pile of meat down behind the post office and into the stand of pines by the highway. There weren't many cars passing through Midville by that time on Christmas Eve. All of the Yankees were already in Florida.

It was dark on the other side of Highway 15, because the moon wasn't shining. The wind was blowing harder, and somewhere in front of us a dog howled.

"I don't know if this is such a good idea, Sissy," Polly whispered. "It's awful scary back here."

"Just don't talk about it. We'll be through in no time. Look, there's the campfire."

The fire blazed, sending little sparks of light like stars up into the black sky. Polly's steps slowed down. To our right side a howl blasted our ears, and we both jumped back so fast, we almost dropped the tray.

"Who's there?" a voice called out from behind a light that bobbed back and forth in the darkness.

The metal tray sent a cloud of dust above our knees when it hit the dirt.

"A-A-Amy Claire, m'am," my voice squeaked out.

"Ah, Sissy is it? What a pleasant Christmas surprise!" It was Madame Margo's voice. Her face blinked light and dark because of the lantern she held above her head as she came toward us.

"Look, look what the child has brought!" She called to the others who began to gather around.

"Blessed Mary, look at those hams," the other Gypsies said. "Where'd you get this pig, girl?"

Polly and I both took a step backward.

"It's your Christmas dinner, j-just like I promised. M-my granddaddy cooked it. Can I get my name back now, please, m'am?"

The crowd closed in tighter. The dogs began to bark again, and the wind blew harder.

"Well, I'll be—" Madame Margo started, letting out a hoot of laughter that brought goose pimples to my arms. Polly and I turned toward each other at the same time.

"Run!" I whispered, and we did. We ran faster than the wind, faster than the dogs that chased after us, and faster even than those Gypsies who followed, shouting, "Wait, wait, come back!"

We scooted across the highway and through the woods, not stopping to catch our breaths until we reached the post office.

"I've gotta go home, Sissy. I'll see you tomorrow," Polly panted. She didn't even wait for me to beg her to stay; she just turned and ran off into the dark.

The lights on Granny's Christmas tree twinkled in the window at the front of the house. As quietly as I could, I slipped through the door and made my way to the kitchen. Elease had gone home for the night, but Granny and Mama were still icing cakes.

"Where've you been, Sissy? Carson junior went to sleep callin' for you."

"Uh, just messin' around with Polly, Mama," I said.

Granny gave me one of her looks, but I stared right back at her. She could tell an all-out lie in a minute, but since what I had told them was just a round-about-truth answer, I was pretty sure I could get away with it.

"Well, now," she said to me, looking over the top of her glasses, "you just quit your messin' around and take this coffee out to Big Daddy and Tyrus. They'll be needin' it to finish up with the pig tonight."

The heat from the coffeepot steamed up the cold air outside, and the wind blew it warm against my face as I walked out to the pit. I heard low talking as I got nearer. I could tell Tyrus's voice right away, and Big Daddy's laugh was the only one in the world that rumbled out low and hoarse like that, but

I heard other voices too soft to make out. It was dark except for a small circle of light from the fire and the one lantern that burned, so I couldn't see who stood on the other side of the pit.

As I walked closer, Big Daddy mumbled something, then he and Tyrus turned toward me. The other voices hushed. I thought I heard the tinkling of bells out in the darkness, but Big Daddy's voice covered up the noise before I could be sure.

"What are you doin' out here this time of night, girl?" he asked.

"I brought y'all some fresh coffee," I answered, straining to see past him into the night. Those bells had reminded me of the Gypsies.

"Well, we sho' do 'preciate that, now don't we, Tyrus. Looks like we're gonna need plenty of coffee if we're goin' to have any kind of Christmas dinner ready by tomorrow. Ain't that right, Tyrus?"

"Yessa, that sho' is right. We got a powerful lot of cookin' yet to do!" Tyrus chuckled way down in his throat. "Seems like our pig heah's done shrunk all up."

I swallowed hard, waiting for them to ask me about the pig. But Big Daddy and Tyrus went on joking about the cooking. I wanted to tell Big Daddy the truth, but I couldn't be sure he would understand. He was too crazy about Carson junior for me to take the chance of telling him about the hex, so I handed him the coffeepot and said good night.

Lying in bed, I listened as the wind rattled the storm shutters. Somewhere in the dark, dogs howled, and I thought of the Gypsies and their dogs. They'd be eating Big Daddy's pig pretty soon. My stomach growled when I wondered what we would eat. It was the worse Christmas Eve ever.

At the first sign of morning my little sisters woke me up to open presents. My new bike was there all right—a shiny purple-and-silver Schwinn with a wire basket on the front. The only disappointment was our stockings. Instead of the candy we usually got, the bulges turned out to be oranges and tangerines from Florida. But we were happy with the other presents, and before long the smells of our Christmas dinner filled the house.

Granny's good china was spread out all along her favorite tablecloth. The glasses and silver sparkled, and everything looked real special. After the blessing, Granny rang the little glass bell by her plate, and Big Daddy left the room and then marched back to the table holding a covered silver platter straight out in front of him. He made a fuss about putting it down just so in front of his place at the table and then picked up the long carving knife, scraping it back and forth across the edge of the meat fork.

"Ah, go on with your showin' off, Bill," Granny laughed. "We're hungry!"

Big Daddy grinned and moved his eyebrows up and down while he smacked his lips.

"Ta-daa!" he sang as he lifted the lid. There in the center of that platter was a fat brown goose!

I've never heard so many people suck in air at one time.

"Bill, you didn't! How could you? Where is the pig?" Granny cried out.

I knew there was gonna be trouble for sure. Granny was going to give Big Daddy down-the-country for what he had done, and it was all my fault. Everything was my fault—Carson junior's hex, Queenie's murder, and now my own Big Daddy was going to get blamed for losing the Christmas dinner that I had stolen.

"G-G-Granny," I stuttered. "It's—it's . . ."

"Ho, dere! Anybody home dis mornin'?" Tyrus's voice called out from the kitchen door.

"Tyrus! We're just about to enjoy this fine Christmas goose you and I cooked up last night. Come and have some," Big Daddy laughed.

"Ah, and a fine fat goose she is all right, Mr. Bill," Tyrus answered. His grin was the first part of him to come into the room. "Merry Christmas, y'all! How's everyone? Looks like y'all eatin' good today, huh?" Tyrus laughed again. "I can't stay now. Jus' wanted to wish everybody a fine Christmas day! How 'bout it now, Santa Claus good to ya?"

Tyrus patted my head with his cold hand. "Got that new bicycle you been wantin' so, Sissy?"

I nodded and dropped my head down so Tyrus couldn't see the tears filling up my eyes.

"Well, ain't dat jus' fine—everythin' workin' out so good and all. I bes' be goin' now. I'll see y'all a little later on."

Tyrus started out the door with his chuckling, but then stopped and turned back toward Big Daddy. "Oh, yeah, I 'bout forgot, Mr. Bill. Ya know dat Queenie you been wantin' to catch? Well, I gots her out back in de pen fer ya. De cold weather slowed her down a bit, I reckon. Caught her early dis mornin' afore she could get too quick

on her legs. Y'all have a good day now, heah?" He
patted my head again as he left.

Big Daddy held his sides laughing at our surprised faces, and Granny threw her napkin at him.
"Oh, you old fool," she laughed. "Scarin' us like
that!"

Christmas dinner turned out to be just fine. We
even ate some of the rib meat from the pig, but Big
Daddy never did tell why we didn't have ham or
where the goose came from. Every now and then
during dinner he'd look over at me and wink, but
I thought he just felt bad for worrying me about
killing Queenie. It wasn't until later that I found out
what was really going on.

I was showing Polly how to ride my new bike
when he called me out to Queenie's new pen.

"I got a little present for you that I didn't want
the others to see, honey." Big Daddy held my hand
with one of his and slipped his other hand into his
coat pocket. He placed something soft in my palm,
and when I looked down, there was Madame
Margo's black pouch. So it *had* been those Gypsies
out in the dark, I thought.

"Looks like you made a good bargain after all, little girl. A name's worth a whole lot more than a few

hams. Just you remember that now, ya heah, Miss Amy Claire?"

Big Daddy patted my head just like Tyrus had done. I stood for a long time holding that little bag before I had the courage to open it. When at last I did open it, there was nothing inside.

"Polly," I yelled across the yard. She rode up on my bike, popping the brake against the hard dirt, making the tires spin and squeal like crazy. "Look!" I whispered, showing her the pouch. We stood there wondering about those Gypsies and what they had done.

"Well, what am I s'posed to call you now?" Polly asked.

A ball rolled across the dirt between us. Carson junior waddled over from the back steps. "Thithy," he called. "Thithy!"

I knelt down to hand him his ball.

"My name is Amy Claire," I said, holding up the little pouch for him to see.

Carson junior patted his hands together and reached for the little bag. I held it higher.

"AMY CLAIRE!" I spit the name out between my teeth.

He frowned and stamped his foot, and then

reached up with his hand to touch my cheek. His blue eyes seemed darker and bigger than before.

"Thithy," he whispered again quietly, and walked away.

"Oh, no, Polly!" I groaned. "He's still hexed!"

"Ha-ha!" she laughed. "Those Gypsies sure got you good!"

Polly climbed back onto my bike and took off out of the yard, calling back to me over her shoulder, "See ya later—Sissy!"

The Girl
Who Ate Chicken Feet

They said I was unforgivably rude, and they put me on two weeks of restriction for doing it, but I don't care. I'm ten years old and I already know all about the rules girls have to remember, so when I broke 'em, I knew exactly what I was doing.

Me and my cousin Delores were helping Granny make her seven-layer, chocolate rainbow cake. Both of us had three layers to color, and each layer was different. There was a red one, a blue one, then green, yellow, orange, and a special purple one. Delores always said that she was the one who figured out how to make purple, but she was just being her old bossy, braggy self. She knew I was the one who did it. Granny made the last layer brown, to match the chocolate icing we put all over the top, and just as we finished, my mama and Granny's friend Miss Viola came in. We were getting ready to have a snack when Granny thought she heard something at the screen door.

"Sissy, go see if somebody's knockin'. Delores can help serve the cake," Granny said to me.

Just because she was two months older than me, Delores always got to show off for company, but I didn't argue with Granny.

I got a good running start and then slid on my socks about halfway down the fresh-waxed hall, almost all the way to the screen door. I slung that squeaky old thing wide open and stood there staring at the most beautiful lady I had ever seen. She had long, shiny, golden hair, and her eyes were the color of my blue crayon. Her dress was lavender, like the eggs we hide on Easter mornings, and it looked all soft and silky. I thought she might be one of those secret angels God sometimes sends down to earth, because she looked just like one of the pictures in my Sunday-school book. I knew she wasn't from our town; nobody from here looked like her. We have those short, frizzy perm 'dos, and we wear what Mama calls practical polyesters.

Anyway, there she stood on Granny's front porch, looking like one of God's choir members—her hair shining and those eyes looking right at me.

"Is Miss Amelia in, please?" her whispery voice sang.

I couldn't say a word! I just stood there staring, with my mouth hanging open and my eyes bulging out. Granny walked up behind me just then, and she let out this "Great Lord, bless us!" right in my ear. She almost smushed me into the screen door when she reached for that angel. Granny sounded so happy, but then she started to cry and carry on with "Praise the Lord, look who's here!" The crying kind of scared me, because Granny doesn't ever cry. I wondered if this angel visiting us meant that Granny might be greeting God soon, and I looked around for that flash of lightning to come down from heaven and make both of them disappear like in that famous twinkling-of-an-eye thing they talk about in the Bible. But neither one of them went anywhere. They just stood there holding on to each other, crying and smiling, all at the same time.

"What's wrong, Granny?" Delores's mouth yelled from the kitchen.

But Granny didn't answer. She backed me into the screen again when she pulled that angel into the room and led her down the hall. I followed close behind and ducked between Granny and the doorjamb into the kitchen to see what would happen next. Mama and Miss Viola didn't say a word at first, but all of a sudden they were jumping up out of their chairs, crying and laughing and hugging this angel just like Granny had done. Delores gave me one of our secret signs—the high-eyebrow look—and we took our cake and scrunched into the corner by the stove to listen.

"Who's that?" Delores asked, spitting chocolate crumbs all over my face.

I really wanted to tell her this big lie about the angel being a rich relative on my daddy's side of the family, but I just couldn't think fast enough. I love getting one over on her like that, but I didn't have any idea who this person was. It did make me feel better, though, that Delores didn't know her either.

"Just shut up, Delores, so we can hear," I fussed at her.

And that's when I broke the first rule—I sat there and just stared at this angel. I didn't even try to hide it under sideways looks, because I thought

the grown-ups wouldn't notice. They were all staring too.

When all the hugging and crying was over,
Granny said, "Nancy Rae Stoker! I can't believe it!
Lord, it's been nearly twenty years, and just look at
you! You sho' don't look like the same little girl that
left here."

When I heard that name, my chocolate cake got
stuck in my throat, and I went into a coughing spell
right then. Nancy Rae Stoker was an ugly, old witch
that had stared at me for five years from all the dark
doors in my nightmares. This just couldn't be her!
From all the stories I had heard, she had to be some
old, rotten corpse by now, after what she had done.

I looked over at Delores to see if she had caught
the name, but she was too busy stuffing her mouth
with another piece of cake. She doesn't pay attention very long to anything but herself, and she for-
gets a lot of important stuff.

But I remembered all those stories the grown-ups
had told about Nancy Rae and that Great Depression. Granny said back when the Depression was
dying down, people in little towns, especially in the
South, still had the fear of it coming back down on
them. Money wasn't spent too much, but charity

was something that everybody kind of took as their duty to folks who still weren't doing so good. People just tried to help out others who needed food or maybe hand-me-downs to wear. They even made up jobs for them to do: Sometimes it would be raking the dirt driveway so it was all ripply like corduroy material, or maybe they'd just have them count all the empty canning jars in the outside shed. Granny said any old job would do, so that the people could keep something she called their dignity. That was real important back then.

My mama was a teenager when all this was going on in Midville, and Nancy Rae was about nine. Nancy Rae's mama died trying to have another baby, and nobody knew how to find Nancy Rae's daddy, so she had to come live with her cousins. There were four children in that family already, and the cousins didn't really want any more to feed. But they had to take in the orphan because of what people would say if they didn't. So the cousins fixed up the lean-to shed outside of their kitchen for Nancy Rae.

That lean-to is still there. One time I heard my mama say it looked just the same as when Nancy Rae slept in it, so I snuck over there to see for my-self. It's built around the kitchen chimney, and the sides are made of old pieces of tin. There's a bunch of rusty nail holes all over it, and the ends of the nails stick out in the inside where Nancy Rae slept. Mama said Nancy Rae's cousins put up pieces of cardboard to help keep out some of the wind in the winter, and I guess the chimney kept it sort of warm when there was fire in the kitchen stove. But just thinking about how hot it must have been in the summer made me start to sweat, and then Granny's voice pulled me back to our kitchen.

"Lord bless you, child, you sure have changed. You were skinny as switchin' sticks when you left here."

That was pretty hard for me to believe, because the switching sticks I'm used to come off our old willow tree. They're R-E-A-L skinny, and they sting your legs like bees when they snap back real fast against your skin.

"But I'd know those eyes anywhere," Granny went on. "You always did have the bluest eyes."

Granny didn't tell what she always said about those eyes being so sad, they just broke her heart to look at them. She used to say how Nancy Rae came by to sit on the porch with her and shell peas and beans. Granny sat in the old wooden rocker and Nancy Rae sat on the top step, and they sang hymns all afternoon. When all the beans and peas were shelled, Granny gave Nancy Rae a little money, and she never let her leave without first making her eat something, because all the neighbors knew that Nancy Rae didn't get much to eat except for table scraps and fried chicken feet.

When I first heard that, I thought they were lying for sure, but I asked around and I found out they weren't. Times were real hard back then. Granny said that the president wanted everybody to have a chicken in their pot, and this made a real big impression on her. She thought she would do good by raising some of those chickens for the president to buy, but when the president didn't buy them, she sold them to the neighbors, including Nancy Rae's cousins. Most people could only afford to buy one chicken at a time, and one chicken didn't go very far in a big family, so Nancy Rae had to eat the feet.

That just about made me throw up when I heard it, because everybody knows chickens are dumb and dirty. You can't live around them and not know it. They peck and scratch at everything in sight. Then they poop all over the place and peck at the poop. What they don't eat they walk in, so they always have these greenish-yellow globs stuck on their feet. I sure wouldn't want to eat those feet.

When it's time to start dinner at our house, Granny always sends us children out to help Elease get the chicken ready for cooking. We have to chase that chicken all over the yard to catch it. Then Elease holds it by the neck and swings it 'round and 'round in circles until the neck just pops loose from the body. We always laugh when that headless chicken runs 'round the yard with the blood spurting out all over its feet and on the ground. It's just too dumb to know it's dead yet. When it finally does flop over, Elease chops off those nasty chicken feet, and then she throws the chicken into a big pot of boiling water to make it easier to pluck out all the feathers. We always have fried chicken to eat, but we NEVER, NEVER, NEVER EAT THE FEET! We give those to the pigs, along with the head, but poor Nancy Rae had to eat the nasty things or else go hungry, they said.

Anyway, because I knew all this stuff about chickens, I thought Nancy Rae must have died a long time ago. Once I heard Granny telling Miss Viola about some man who got a germ bug in his insides from eating dirty food and he died. So I figured Nancy Rae must have got at least a bad case of worms from those nasty chicken feet, and she must have just rotted away. But now here she was, sitting at our kitchen table, looking like she probably didn't even know what chicken feet were.

Delores was still feeding her face, so when the grown-ups all started asking Nancy Rae questions about what had been happening to her, I slid out of the chair and sat on the floor next to the icebox so I could hear better. Those blue eyes of Nancy Rae's stared out the window toward where those cousins used to live, and then her whispery voice said, "When I got so sick with that fever, Dr. Downing told my cousins I needed lots of rest and good food, but they said they couldn't afford it." Then she giggled and looked over at Granny. "Miss Amelia, do you remember how Dr. Downing used to puff out his chest like a rooster and how his bald head would get real red when he got mad?"

Everybody at the table laughed, and Nancy Rae went on. "Well, he got very upset with the cousins that day, and when he came back two days later, he told me he had found Mama's brother over in Columbia and that I would be going there to live."

Nancy Rae looked at Granny. I could see Nancy Rae real clear; she had tears in her eyes, but she went on talking just the same.

"I never got to thank you for the chicken soup you brought me those next few days. I never even got to say good-bye to you."

Granny didn't say anything. She looked down at her apron and picked at the chocolate icing smeared all over it. I thought for sure she would tell Nancy Rae how everybody in town talked bad about those cousins after that, but she didn't, and the whole room filled up with the quiet. I keep meaning to ask Granny why grown-ups tell you to be quiet, but then when it gets quiet like that day in the kitchen, they act like they can't wait to fill it up with words—like Miss Viola did. She started telling Nancy Rae about Granny's recipe for chicken soup, and everybody said how good it is, but thinking about it made my stomach start to gurgle.

Granny finally looked up to say, "I wish I could have said good-bye to you too, Nancy Rae."

She didn't tell her that the neighbors had heard the terrible fight that went on when Nancy Rae's uncle came to get her and how, after that, when anybody asked the cousins about Nancy Rae, those cousins acted like they were ignoring somebody's bad manners and wouldn't say a word! 'Course, nobody around the table told Nancy Rae about that either.

Nancy Rae went on with her story. "It took me a while to get over the rheumatic fever," she said, and it sounded to me like she called it room-attic fever. But I bet she got it sleeping in that lean-to off the kitchen.

And what Nancy Rae said next really got everybody to talking. "I finished high school and worked my way through college. I'm working for the state now, counseling abused children."

You should have heard all the "I'll bes" and the "ain't that somethings" going on around our kitchen table when she said that.

But then that awful quiet came in the room again when Nancy Rae said, "Sometimes I cry over them. I know how they feel."

The grown-ups all looked at each other, and then real quick somebody filled in the space again by saying how the weather was looking pretty bad outside.

Delores got up and prissed around serving more cake, and the grown-ups told Nancy Rae about everybody that had died and about all the babies that had been born. I could tell Nancy Rae was trying to follow the rule about listening politely, but pretty soon she said she had to leave because it did look like a storm was coming up.

We all followed Nancy Rae out to her car, and I was trying to stay close so I could hear everything, but Delores pushed herself right up in front of me. Everybody hugged Nancy Rae, even Delores, and told her to come back again real soon. Then Granny reached for her, and Nancy Rae made a wet, choking kind of sound—like she was trying real hard not to cry, but I couldn't get close enough to see if she was or not.

When she got in her car, all I could think about was that Nancy Rae was leaving and I probably wouldn't ever get to see her again, so right then and there I decided to break another rule. I pushed through Delores and the grown-ups to the side of Nancy Rae's car. I just wanted to tell her we sure were sorry about all the bad things in her life. For a minute I couldn't talk at all, and when my voice finally did work, what blurted out was, "I'm real sorry you had to eat all those chicken feet when you were little, Nancy Rae."

There was quiet again, but this time I knew what would fill it up just as soon as Nancy Rae left. That angel Gabriel wouldn't have gotten any more looks than me if he had shown up to blow his horn right then. I heard my mama say, "Oh, dear Lord!" and

when I looked at her, her face was as red as toma-
toes. Granny's mouth was hanging open; Delores
fell down on the grass laughing and pointing her finger at me, and Miss Viola looked up in the trees and
down the street like she had lost something important.

I thought about trying to explain. I knew it wasn't
polite to mention somebody's terrible troubles, but
I really wanted Nancy Rae to know that she hadn't
eaten all those chicken feet for nothing. After meeting her and all, I was really glad she wasn't dead
in the ground like I had always thought. It seemed to
me that she might want to know somebody was glad
she hadn't died from all that stuff, even if it did
mean I had to break the rules to say it. But I didn't
try to explain. My mouth was too dry, and I felt like
if I tried to make it work, I might start crying. The
worst part was going to be listening to Delores's
teasing and hearing her brag about how she knew
how to act around grown-ups and I didn't. She was
still over there just laughing at me, and I wished real
hard that she would wet her pants.

Nancy Rae wasn't laughing at me, though. She
got out of her car and gave me a big hug, right in
front of everybody.

"Thanks, Sissy," she said. "And just so you'll

know the whole story—I really just ate the batter from around those chicken feet."

Nancy Rae left then, and the good-bye smile on Mama's face disappeared the minute she looked at me. She went down the whole list of things you don't say to people and ended up like always with how sometimes she didn't even recognize me, her own child. But it was all worth it in the end—what with Nancy Rae's hug and her telling me the truth about those chicken feet, and the very best thing of all was when Delores really did wet her pants!

Crazy Saree

She was a bent, scarred old beggar who showed up at our back-door steps every Wednesday at noon when the cotton gin whistle blew. Nobody paid much attention to her, but we always knew when she was coming, because the kids in town followed her around singing that singsong rhyme they made up about her.

> *"Crazy Saree, ugly and hairy,*
> *She's an old witch, mean and scary."*

When she heard that, Crazy Saree reared her head back, howling "Ah-oooh!" and shook the crooked tree branch she used as a walking stick high in the

air to chase them away. Then she'd make her way,
slow and cripplelike, up to Granny's porch steps.

It must have taken her a long time to walk the
two blocks from the cotton gin to Granny's house.
She toted all the stuff she owned in the world inside
a dirty feed sack that hung over her shoulder and
down her humped-up back. That walking stick
didn't seem strong enough to stand the weight of
her and the sack, but it never broke. The older kids
said it was a magic stick, and that if you got too
close to Crazy Saree, she'd say some magic words
to change it into a snake that would run you down
dead in the road. Then you'd get stuffed in that
sack of hers and eaten up piece by piece along with
the fish heads they said she hauled around.

The last time she came wasn't a bit different.
The kids chased her, and Crazy Saree howled all the
way to Granny's back porch. Her stick pounded on
the frame of the screen door, *bam-a-lam-a-lam!*

"Wanna s'change some kindlin' fer some food,"
she growled.

"It's been waitin' on you, Saree," Granny answered, and she brought out a tin plate piled high
with food. Crazy Saree sat on the top step with her
back against the porch column and her legs spread

wide to hug the feed sack. Her stick stretched across her knees like a crooked bridge.

I liked how she slurped her food from the spoon and then mushed it between her black gums.

"Meat's too tough. Rice's too dry," she grumbled.

"Well, that's all right, Saree," Granny answered. "You just eat what you can and don't worry about leavin' the kindlin'."

Crazy Saree didn't worry about the kindling either. She grunted back at Granny, sucked the meat bones clean, and then tossed them to the yard dogs. She drained the sweet tea from the jar, burped out loud, smacked her lips, and set the empty dish and jar on the steps. Then she pushed herself up off the steps, slung her sack over her shoulder again, and hobbled away.

That last time she came, I followed her when she left. 'Course, I stayed way back so she wouldn't know I was there, and when she turned down the trail that led into the swamp, I ducked from bush to bush trying to hide. Every now and then Crazy Saree stopped and let out her "Ah-oooh!" breaking up the quiet. The farther we went into the swamp, the darker it got under the cypress trees. The rustlings and chirpings sounded almost as loud as her howls. I kept thinking I should turn back, but it was like I was hypnotized by her. I just had to know where she was going. Nobody else knew where Crazy Saree lived, and that would be something to brag about.

Pretty soon we came to a clearing at the edge of the water, and Crazy Saree swung her sack and walking stick onto the soggy ground. The sack made a heavy-sounding thump; then whatever was inside of it settled into a different shape against a big rock. Crazy Saree bent over it, but I couldn't see what she pulled out. From behind her it looked like she hugged something, and her body rocked back and forth. First I heard just a soft humming, but then I heard the words to the same lullaby Granny used to sing to me, and the quiet around the clearing filled up with Crazy Saree's voice. My eyes got all watery.

I must have breathed loud, because the singing stopped real quick and Crazy Saree grabbed her stick and turned toward where I was hiding behind a clump of cattails. She dragged the stick around in a circle across the mud and then pointed it right at me, shouting, "I knows you, chile!"

I didn't wait to hear what else she said. Her horrible "Ah-oooh!" chased me into the sunlight outside of the swamp.

*   *   *

I didn't tell anybody what I had seen, but I thought about Crazy Saree a lot that next week. I even asked Granny and Elease about her, but they both gave me the same answer: "Just you leave Saree alone now, you heah? She's got enough troubles."

I wanted to ask about those troubles, but I knew they would wonder why I was asking, so I just kept quiet and waited for her to come back the next Wednesday. I thought maybe I would follow her again.

But Crazy Saree never came back.

"Wonder what happened to Saree today. She's never missed her dinner before," Granny said to Elease. I could tell Granny was worried, because she found a lot to do out in the backyard that afternoon, and she even walked down to the post office instead of sending me like she usually did.

"Nobody's seen her around these last two days," I heard her telling Elease when she got back.

That's when I got the idea to go find Crazy Saree myself. I didn't tell Granny I was going. She'd want to know how I knew where to look, and then I'd get in trouble for going there the first time. Granny would fuss about how my curiosity is more than ten people ought to have. So I left the house without telling anybody where I was going, and I followed the trail just like before. When I got to the clearing at the edge of the water, I found her.

She was on her side, curled around the big rock, and those crooked fingers of hers still held on to that dirty sack. She was definitely dead. The bottoms of her feet looked like lizard skin, and the toes were long and skinny, reminding me of fingers, with nails that were thick like the ones on hunting dogs. Her nails were real yellow, the color of dried mustard, and they curled around and under the ends of her toes. It must have hurt to walk on those feet, and I think that must have been why she limped along with her crooked stick.

I couldn't stand being there by myself looking at Crazy Saree. Sweat dripped down my sides even though it was cool in the swamp, and my knees shook. My breath was puffing in and out so fast that little dark spots floated in front of my eyes. Night was coming, and the swamp was scary enough in the daylight. I didn't want to be alone with a dead crazy person. I didn't know how I was going to explain to Granny about being in Three Hole Swamp and finding Crazy Saree. She was going to say my curiosity got the best of me this time for sure. But I knew I had to tell her, and so I did.

The nightmares started that night, and I was back in the swamp just like I had been for real that afternoon. In my dreams I found Crazy Saree lying dead by that big rock, only she didn't stay dead. I bent over to look at her and poke her on the shoulder, and she jerked up yelling "Ah-oooh!" and reached out with her long crooked stick to hit me.

"I knows you, chile. I knows you!" she screeched over and over while she stuffed me into her old sack. Her hands pushed me down and down inside of it. I couldn't breathe because the bag smelled like the sour dirt underneath old houses. I felt all cramped up and closed in too—a smothery kind of feeling. In the dreams I kept trying to get a big suck of air in, but I couldn't get enough. I tried to push myself out of the sack, but my arms and legs felt like they were made of cement. They wouldn't move. Just when I thought I was going to die if I didn't get a good big breath, I woke up screaming. It was a terrible, scary kind of dream. It made me throw up.

After the second night Granny came up with a plan.

"Sissy, we're going to see Saree at the funeral home. I need to see to the arrangements."

"But, Granny—"

Granny turned to me and held my face between her hands, so I had to look right into those eyes of hers that always saw everything.

"And you need to see Saree," she said.

I choked down my cereal and even though the cold air outside felt good on my face, my cereal didn't want to stay down. My feet weren't in any hurry to get there either, but I followed Granny to the colored people's funeral home behind the firehouse.

Two big wooden doors opened into this dark, skinny hall, and inside, everything was brown. The floors, the walls, and even the ceilings were covered with dark, thick wood. When the doors creaked shut behind us, my stomach turned over again, and my mouth worked hard to breathe the air my nose couldn't. It smelled like the back of old closets and tasted like gas.

"Mornin', Miz 'Melia. You come about Saree?"

"Mornin', Hiram. Yes we did. Reverend Johnson said he would meet us this mornin' to finalize the funeral plans, but I'd like for Sissy here to see Saree for just a minute if that's all right."

"Sho' is, Miz 'Melia. Saree's had a lot of company already dis morning. Y'all come on down dis way. She's all ready for ya."

Hiram's face was a dusty gray color in the dim light of that hall. He looked like one of those preachers that came through town once in a while to tell about the devil and the fire in hell, only his clothes didn't fit exactly right. His arms and legs hung out from under his coat and pants, and when he took us down the hall to see the body, he had to duck underneath the lightbulbs that dangled from string cords hanging from the ceiling.

Crazy Saree's body was waiting in a room at the end of the hall. The room was dark except for a few candles next to the casket. I stepped on Granny's heel as I followed her into the room.

"Here, Sissy, let me hold your hand," she whispered, and she held it just tight enough. Granny always knew what I needed.

The air was different in this room. It smelled too sweet, like cherry syrup. There was no noise at all, except my breathing. I guess the quiet settled me down a little, because while Granny prayed, my curiosity came back, and I peeped through my eyelashes to get a good look at Crazy Saree.

"She doesn't look like Crazy Saree, Granny. I never saw her smile," I whispered to Granny after she finished her praying.

Saree's hands were folded prayerlike across a flowered dress, but those crooked fingers were the same ones that had been holding on to that lumpy sack when I found her. I couldn't see her feet in the coffin because that part was shut, but I'll never forget how they looked before. The thought brought back my sweat and chills. I was just about to ask Granny if we could leave when Hiram came into the room.

"Miz 'Melia? De reverend's on his way. Y'all can wait in de office if you want."

"Let Sissy go on in there, Hiram, and I'll be along in a little while."

Hiram took me back down the skinny hall and opened the door to another dark room. He pointed to a chair, turned on a small desk lamp, and smiled on his way out, closing the door behind him.

I watched the clock pendulum swing back and forth; the ticking sounded loud and hollow in the quiet of that room. My fingers traced the cracks in the leather on the chair while I sat there waiting, just like I was told to do. I got sleepy and was almost dozing off when the clock chimed. The sound bounced off the walls, and then there was just that soft ticking again and the lamplight bouncing off of the pendulum. My sweat dripped down onto the chair arms, and the leather made little sucking noises when I pulled my hands free. I looked around the room, and from a dark corner a shape popped out at me. It was the thing from my nightmares, lying right there on a table! It was Crazy Saree's sack. My heart pounded, and my chest tightened up.

"Please, God, please let me breathe," I prayed.

Sweat rolled down my face and dripped from under my arms, then ran down my sides. My whole body shook. The room began to spin, around and around, faster and faster. I tried to get up out of the chair, but my arms and legs wouldn't work. It was like having that bad dream again, except that I knew I was awake, and that was even worse.

I grunted, hoping the sound would make my body work. I tried to get more air in as the room began to spin again. I was spinning with it, losing my grip on the chair. There was a feeling like falling, but suddenly everything stopped. There were hands on my shoulders and a familiar voice came out of the dark.

"Sissy, Sissy girl, it's Reverend Johnson."

I grabbed for those strong hands and climbed into the waiting arms up to that voice. The arms tightened around me. The hands patted my back.

"It's all right now, Sissy. I gots ya. I gots ya."

The reverend eased himself down into the chair, and I settled in his lap, even though I knew I was getting too big for that sort of thing. He patted my back, holding me close while I gasped for air between sobs. My story came out in mixed-up words. I told him everything: how the kids teased Crazy Saree, how I followed her—spied on her—and then how I found her dead. I told him about the nightmares. Then I pointed to the sack of children's bones.

He moved to reach for it, and my hands slid from behind his neck, one to stop his arm, the other up to his cheek by the corner of his mouth. I could feel his smile, the corner of his mouth pushing into his cheek, the lips curling up and out. But it wasn't a happy smile. A tear rolled down his cheek and between my spread fingers.

"Oh, chile, there ain't nothin' t' fear 'bout ol' Saree's sack."

I didn't believe him. My hands pressed harder against him, and the reverend sighed and settled back against the leather of the chair.

"Sissy, let me tell you 'bout ol' Saree. It ain't nothin' like you chirren think.

"You know, Saree was goin' on seventy-seven years old. She's been walkin' 'round this town for forty years for a very special reason. A long time ago when she was real young, Saree fell in love with a white man. 'Course they didn't get married, but she had a baby by him, a girl named Clarice. The white man left town right after Clarice was born, but Saree worked real hard to give Clarice a good home. She cooked and cleaned for all the white people in town, and she used the money to buy pretty dresses for her little girl. Clarice grew up to be beautiful—dark curly hair, big green eyes, and skin that was the color of honey. Folks thought Clarice was real special.

"But when Clarice got to be a teenager, Saree used to tell me every Sunday, 'Lord, Reverend. Ya need to pray for my baby girl. She's done changed on me. She's wild, Reverend. Won't listen to nothin' I tells her. She's hangin' 'round with a rough bunch of white boys from that loggin' camp down near de river. They come by in their cars and take Clarice off to juke joints, and ya know, Reverend, dose ain't no good places fer girls to go.'

"Well, Sissy, I prayed for her. The whole church prayed, but the troubles started gettin' worse. One night when I was over at Saree's, the sheriff came to talk to her. He says, 'Saree, we think those loggin' men are breakin' into places and robbin' people. You need to keep Clarice away from 'em.'

"Saree did try, but Clarice was just plain hard-headed. An' 'bout a week later the sheriff was back."

The reverend took a deep breath, and then he went on with the story.

"The sheriff said those men had shot and killed somebody, and the talk 'round town was that Clarice was a witness. Said he needed to talk to her 'bout it.

"But Clarice wasn't home—she hadn't come home at all the night before, and po' ol' Saree was scared for her.

"So then the sheriff, he got up a search party, and me and your granddaddy went off lookin' toward Three Hole Swamp. Some folks said those loggers used to party down at a clearin' there. Could be, we thought, they was all down there drinkin' and car-ryin' on. So we took off to look there first. We didn't know Saree followed us.

"It was gettin' on kind of late in the day when we got back up near the water. Right there where you found Saree lyin' dead is where we found Clarice's body. Me and your granddaddy was just turnin' to fire the signal shots when Saree busted out of the woods.

"'Fore we could stop her, she threw herself down over Clarice, and when we tried to pull her up, she just went wild. She grabbed up a broke tree branch and made us back away.

"'I told her 'bout that white trash,' she cried. 'Now they done beat her up and busted open her head. Oh, Lord, my chile, my chile. Get back! You two just get back! Leave me be. Leave me be. I gots to take care of my baby!'

"Me and your granddaddy walked down the trail to meet the sheriff. We thought it best to give Saree some time alone with Clarice before all the others came up. Couldn't have been gone more than an hour at most, but when we came back, Saree and Clarice were gone.

"Nobody 'round town saw Saree for a long time after that. When she finally did come back, she was changed all 'round. She wouldn't go back to live at her house. She wouldn't talk much to people. When they asked about Clarice's body, Saree said, 'Me and God done took care of it. Just you leave me 'lone.' Then she threw back her head and howled, wavin' that stick of hers high in the air.

"Two bodies floated up in the swamp about a month later. Folks thought they might've been two of the men with the loggin' crew, but that company had moved on, and nobody knew for sure. Saree wouldn't say nothin' when you asked her 'bout it.

People didn't know what to do. The sheriff finally decided it best to just leave her be, and so we did— we just leave her be."

When Reverend Johnson stopped talking, his cheeks were wet, and so were mine. I thought about the sack again, and he must have felt me stiffen up, because he squeezed me close and patted my back some more. I could hear his heart going *ca-thump, ca-thump,* real slow and easy under my head. I could smell the tobacco and Old Spice man-smell that was so much like my granddaddy's.

"Reverend Johnson, do you think Clarice's bones are in Saree's sack?"

The reverend hugged me real close.

"Now, Sissy, you don't really b'lieve that, do you, chile? Let's me and you look, okay? Come on now. You knows I ain't goin' to let nothin' scare you."

He led me over to where the sack slumped in bulges and lumps across the tabletop. I held my breath and watched him untie the unraveling rope that held the sack closed. When he stuck one of his hands down in it, my breath stopped again. Out came a pile of old faded clothes and a pair of men's boots that had holes in the bottoms. There was a piece of cardboard stuck down inside each of them. I breathed.

His hand went in again and came out with a ragged Bible. The black cover was peeling away all along the edges, and when Reverend Johnson opened it up, I could see that some of the pages were torn and others were missing. The Bible looked like it had gotten wet. Right in the middle of it we found a picture of a little girl.

"That's Clarice," the reverend said. He handed the picture to me. She was really pretty, all dressed up in a white dress, her hair curling around her head. She had a big happy smile on her face, like it might have been her birthday or something. She didn't look like the kind of girl to grow up to get herself killed.

Some dried-up flowers fell out from behind the picture, and a little silver cross was stuck deep down in the seam of the Bible, just behind the flowers. It looked like the cross Clarice wore in the picture. I put it back real gentle.

The reverend patted the sack flat on the desk; all the lumps were gone. Then he picked it up, shook it with a snap, and opened it wide so I could see there wasn't anything else in there. I held Saree's Bible while he put the other things back in the sack, and then I laid it carefully on top of the clothes. We tied the rope again, just like it was before, and went outside to sit on the front steps till Granny came out.

The reverend and I didn't talk much while we waited. He smoked on his pipe, and I breathed in the cool fresh air. Somebody was cooking barbecue down the road, and my stomach growled. It had been a long time since breakfast.

Granny came out and talked with the reverend about the afternoon service for Saree. When they finished, Granny and I started to go back home.

" 'Bye, Reverend," I said.

The reverend patted my head and leaned over to whisper in my ear, "Sweet dreams, little Sissy. Sweet dreams."

I saw him at the funeral. The reverend did a real good job by Saree. Just about everybody in town came. I went up to the front of the church with Granny to say good-bye to Saree and saw that someone had put her Bible in her hands, but I didn't see her sack.

Saree's been dead for two weeks now, and I still wonder what happened to her sack. Sometimes late at night I remember the stories about that sack. The only thing that makes those thoughts go away is when I pretend I can hear the reverend's whisper again. Then when I go to sleep, I dream about a little green-eyed girl, all dressed up in white. She stands in front of a birthday cake, and Saree is there too, calling out to me, "I knows you, chile. I knows you."

Chasing Snakes

Big Daddy should have known better than to tell Delores and me that we couldn't go, because Delores can't stand to be told no about anything. As soon as he said that word, she started making plans. She had already made up her mind to go to that Garden of Eden.

Eden is right across the dirt road in front of Granny's house, and people call it Eden because it's just about the prettiest place in the whole world. One day Big Daddy took us grandkids to see it, and I thought the name fit real good. Giant pecan trees grow up on two sides of the garden and make a nice shady spot right in the middle of Mr. Ledger's cornfield. We played there all afternoon, rolling around in the soft clover that grows up a high bank on one side of the clearest blue-water pond you ever saw. On the back side of the pond is a cornfield, and the other side is closed in by Mr. Ledger's chicken houses. But blueberry bushes hide the wire fence around the houses, so the whole place is private, like a real secret garden, all cool and green and leafy. The only problem is that the bottom of that pond drops off sharp and deep, and this little boy drowned in it a while back. Since then, nobody is allowed to go there. But none of that mattered one bit to Delores.

For days we sat on the front steps, looking across the road at Eden, and the thought of going there just about drove Delores crazy. She lived up the road in Huntstown and every summer she'd come stay at Granny's, and every summer it seemed like we always got into trouble because of Delores being so bossy. Granny said Delores got bored living in the country, and that was why she was always carrying on about things, but Granny was just plain wrong about that. Delores wanted to do whatever she wasn't supposed to do, and she thought because she was from the city, she could come to the country and boss the rest of us around. And when she made up her mind to go over to that Garden of Eden, that was that.

I tried to talk her out of it. I told her about how drowned people looked all gray and puffed up and how turtles and fish could take big bites out of your skin. Then I told her there might be more dead people there that hadn't been found yet because nobody ever went over there anymore, but Delores didn't care. Even the blueberry bushes and chicken houses that worked like magnets to draw all kinds of snakes didn't scare her. I thought for sure they would, but she just stomped on my foot and told me to shut up when I tried to tell her about them.

"I'm going, and you're going with me, Sissy. And don't you dare tell Granny or Big Daddy 'cause if you do, I'll make you sorry!"

She would too. I knew all about how sorry Delores could make somebody for doing something she didn't want done—like the time she didn't want to go swimming at the creek, and my friend Polly and I went anyway.

"I'll make y'all sorry," she shouted at us as we left. But when we came home, Delores acted so sweety-sweet to us that we were feeling ashamed that we had left her out of things. She had even made us some chocolate cupcakes, and Polly and I ate two each.

"Y'all like that icing I made?" she giggled.

"Um-huh!" Polly and I answered at the same time.

"Well, that's good, 'cause you're both gonna hate it tomorrow."

"Why?" we asked together, again.

Delores curled her ponytail around one finger and prissed away from us, smiling.

"Because I mixed up some of Granny's chocolate laxative squares in it—that's why!" she yelled over her shoulder.

Sure enough, Polly and I didn't feel good for two days after that.

Anyway, a few days later, our neighbor Mr. Ledger stopped by the house to visit us. Delores and I were napping in the swing on the porch, and I woke up in time to hear Mr. Ledger saying something about a big problem with snakes over at his chicken houses.

"Seems like every time I look out the window, those snakes are droppin' down from the sky—KA-POW-YOW!—crackin' up all my chicken eggs, and I can just see my bank account shrinkin'. I swear those snakes are eatin' me alive, Bill."

When he said that, I punched Delores in the side. She needed to hear about those snakes, but she was sleeping hard, her mouth hanging open and drool sliding down one side of her chin. By the time she woke up, Mr. Ledger and Big Daddy were talk-

ing about something else and she didn't believe me
when I told her what he said. She just put on her
city airs again and sneered at me.

"Mr. Ledger's crazy as a bedbug, Sissy. Snakes
don't eat you alive. They bite you or choke you first.
He's just making up stories again, and you're just a
yellow-bellied chicken about going over there."

But just like Delores didn't believe me, I didn't
believe her either.

Later that night we went to a revival service at the
church, and Reverend Rightner preached about the
Garden of Eden and the serpent of temptation.
When he got to the part about how even little kids
could be chased and hounded by that devil, I punched
Delores, hoping she would pay attention, but right
then the choir started singing "Just As I Am," and
I watched Mr. Ledger and several other people
make their way to the front of the church. I thought
maybe Delores might go up too and get relieved of
that serpent that hounded her, because if ever anybody was hounded by temptation, it was Delores.
But she was busy writing down the names of all the
kids our age that were going up to the altar. Delores
kept lists of everything and everybody.

"You never know when you might need some
of this information," Delores told me, trying to

sound grown-up just because she turned eleven two months before I did. She never did answer the reverend's call that night, and we went home still carrying a heavy burden of sin and Delores's blackmail list.

Early the next morning Delores decided it was time to put her plan to work.

"Sissy, go tell Granny we're going over to Polly's house for a picnic and we won't be back until late. Tell her to fix some lunch to carry with us too."

"Why do I have to do the lyin' all the time, Delores? You go tell her. It's your stupid idea, and you should be the one to lie about it. Granny can always tell when I'm lyin' and then I get in big trouble, and I don't want to go anyway, so this time you just go lie for yourself!"

Delores didn't say anything else; she didn't have to. Before I knew what was happening, she jerked up my arm and pinched me right in that soft spot underneath. Then she gave my arm a hard twist. After I got up from my knees, I went and lied to Granny. I guess I did a pretty good job of it, because she didn't ask any questions. She even fixed us some sandwiches and cherry Kool-Aid to take along.

As soon as Polly met us at the church, Delores took charge. She led us through the cornfield so nobody could see us from the road, and then she shushed us the whole way to Eden when we tried to whisper anything to her—like how she should be walking down the rows and not across them. Finally we just hushed and let Delores make a mess of poor Mr. Ledger's corn.

By the time we got to Eden, black dust covered our feet and legs up to our knees, and sweat dripped off our heads in big plops onto our shirts. It was blazing hot, and I thought about the reverend's talk on the fires of hell burning right here in our town. But then the sight of that cool blue water chased all this right out of my head, and my bad feelings toward Delores changed just a little bit. I even kind of thought maybe this plan of hers might be a good one after all.

Before we could go in the water, though, Delores stood up above us on the bank.

"Okay, y'all, listen up. These are the rules. No screaming, no dunking, especially me 'cause I get an earache, and no going near the drop-off. Y'all have to take turns being lookout. Sissy, you have to be first."

I climbed up the bank, and while Delores and Polly splashed in the pond, I kept watch over the cornfields and the chicken houses. Then when it was my turn to swim, Delores decided it was time for lunch, so we spread our towels on the ground right under the pecan trees and ate our sandwiches. We let the red Kool-Aid dribble from between our lips and pretended to be blood-sucking vampires.

"I wonder if vampires go to hell," I drooled at Polly. "It's not like they wanted to be made into vampires, ya know."

"Yeah, but they kill people, and that means hell," she gurgled back.

"But somebody else causes them to do it. They don't have a choice, Polly. It's kill or die."

"Reverend Rightner said everybody has a choice, Sissy. Even Eve—she should've said no to that serpent."

That reminded me of Mr. Ledger's worries about being eaten up by the chicken snakes, so I started telling Polly what he said on the porch.

"Shut up, Sissy!" Delores growled.

Then Polly told some stories about snakes too, and Delores was getting madder and madder, but I decided I just had to tell Big Daddy's story about the chasing snakes.

"Hey, y'all, Big Daddy says chasin' snakes are long, black, and skinny, and they can hide most anywhere. If you don't look where you're goin', they can pop up their heads from the grass or from be-

hind a bush, or drop down from the trees real quick
to scare you. And as soon as you scream, they'll put
their tails in their mouths and roll like wheels chasin'
right after you. When they catch you, they flatten out
again and use their tails to beat you across the back.
Big Daddy says nobody can outrun a chasin' snake."

Right about then clouds covered up the sun, and
a breeze blew in from across the corn. We all shiv-
ered a little, and Delores jumped up and started
laughing and pointing her finger at me.

"Sissy, you are such a baby to believe Big Daddy's
tall tales. Stop trying to scare us. I know everything
about snakes," she bragged. "If one came along, I'd
use my new karate moves to stomp on its head.
Then I'd grab it by the tail and snap it—quick—just
like a whip and toss it away!" She did some jerky
kind of moves with her arms and legs that she said
were karate, and just when I thought Polly might
start believing her, the tree branch right above Delores's head began to shake. I elbowed Polly and
nodded toward the spot, and we knew right away
what was going to happen. Delores kept on showing
off her karate, thinking we were so impressed, but
we were really watching the long, black body that
was uncurling itself from around the branch and
slowly sliding toward her. The snake's head dangled

just above her ponytail and flicked its tongue in and out a couple of times.

"Uh, Delores, there's a—a snake right over your head."

"Yeah, sure, Sissy, I'm gonna believe you all right," she snarled and went right on bragging and waving her arms and legs all around. Every time she made a new move, the snake weaved back and forth over her head, sliding a little lower with each move. It looked like Delores and that snake were doing some kind of dance, only Delores didn't know she had a partner.

Delores's arms chopped and her legs kicked, all in slow-motion so Polly and I could admire what she called "her style." We smiled and moved with the snake, in and out, back and forth, almost hypnotized.

Polly's "ooh!" broke the trance when two more snakes slid from beneath the leaves to dangle over Delores.

"Delores, for real—three snakes are hangin' over your head, and you better move fast!" I yelled the warning as Polly and I scooted backward across the clover.

"Sissy, I told you to shut up about snakes. I'm not falling for any of your dumb old jokes," she sneered back at me. She moved again to show off some fancy side kick she had made up, and the first snake jerked quick in surprise and slipped completely off the branch and fell, its body landing over Delores's left shoulder and across her back. The other two plopped to the ground and coiled up right by Delores's feet, and then a sound like those demons in hell that the reverend talks about let loose in that secret, quiet garden. I swear those snakes grinned when they heard Delores scream. She tossed the snake off her shoulder, and her arms and legs began pumping up and down like some big train engine. Then she took off running with those snakes rolling over and over like three big bicycle wheels right behind her!

Polly and I followed them down the slope toward the chicken yard. We couldn't believe it when Delores took a big leap over the fence and landed right on top of a bunch of chickens. The chickens put up an awful squawking alarm, and about that time Mr. Ledger's head poked from around the corner of one of the coops.

"Hey, you there—what're you doin' chasing my chickens like that? Stop, you hear me, I said stop!" Mr. Ledger shouted it over and over, but that Delores didn't slow down one bit. She scrambled around on her hands and knees, got her balance, and took off running again. Polly and I ducked down behind a blueberry bush and watched Delores racing

toward home. The snakes had disappeared some-
time during all that noise, and I worried that maybe
they might sneak up on Polly and me, but I knew we
couldn't risk moving.

Polly and I held our breath while we watched Mr.
Ledger pick up two dead chickens that Delores had
squashed, and I knew for sure there was going to be
trouble if he recognized any of us. We stayed behind
that bush until he walked back toward his house.
Then we cut across the cornfield to take the long
way home.

Delores was standing on the front porch when we
reached Granny's house.

"Did I kill any chickens?" she asked.

Polly and I held up two fingers, and Delores's
eyes filled up with tears. She sat down in one of the
rockers, and Polly and I took the swing. The rest of
the afternoon Delores rocked and we swung. We
didn't talk; we just waited to see if Mr. Ledger
would come across the road to tell Granny about
the dead chickens.

He never did come, but at church that night we
worked hard to keep Granny from getting anywhere
too near him. I don't remember much about the
reverend's sermon, but he must have touched Delores's heart, because she went up to the altar that

night, and she tore up her blackmail list when we got home. What's more, she never said or did anything to Polly and me to get even.

Polly and I went back to Eden a lot that summer, but Delores never did, even after we told her what Mr. Ledger said to Big Daddy down at the post office about two weeks after the trip to Eden.

"You still havin' trouble with those snakes, Ledger?" Big Daddy asked him.

"Ya know, it's the darndest thing, Bill. About two weeks ago I was out in the chicken yard cleanin' up a bit, when this child come tearin' across the field from over at the pond with these three big snakes chasin' right behind. I ain't never heard such a commotion. She was screamin' like a banshee when she jumped the fence, and 'fore I could stop her, she raced away and just plain disappeared. Must've been all that screamin' that did the trick, or maybe she just ran those snakes to death, 'cause I ain't seen any snakes since!"

"Never heard of anybody outrunnin' a chasin' snake," Big Daddy laughed. Mr. Ledger winked at Polly and me. I'm still not sure whether or not he knew it was us that day in Eden, but one thing's for sure—Delores did prove Big Daddy was wrong about chasing snakes—she could outrun 'em.

Making Miracles

"Get on your knees and lay yourselves down before God Almighty. We're goin' to make a miracle today!"

Delores sounded just like a preacher up there on the pulpit.

"We shouldn't be in here, Delores. We're goin' to get caught for sure. Please, don't make us do this. It's stupid, and it ain't gonna work."

"You just hush up, Sissy, and start praying. I'm getting that baby sister, and you and Polly are going to help me. Now get to it!"

I wanted to go home. Delores hadn't explained exactly what this miracle plan of hers was, but I had the feeling that it would get us into big trouble. My hands and knees were already full of the splinters that I got when Delores shoved me across the windowsill to break into the church. They stung even against the velvet kneeling cushions at the altar. But that didn't matter to her. Delores was determined to try her new scheme to get a baby sister, but Polly and I thought God must not want her to have one, because none of her other plans had worked. She tried everything she could think of to convince her mama, including leaving notes on her bed pillow.

> *Dear Boo,*
> *Your little girl needs a sister to play with.*
> *Please have a baby soon.*
> *Signed,*
> *Someone Who Cares*

But the notes didn't work. Aunt Boo was playing in a band called The Ladies' Afternoon Old-Time Boogie-Woogie Band, and she didn't want to give it up. She loved playing the boogie-woogie on the piano. That was how she got her name "Boo" a long time ago, and it didn't look as if she was going to give up her music just to make Delores happy.

So, when her notes didn't work, Delores had Polly and me praying in the bedroom three times a day, and now she wanted us to break into the church. I guess she thought she was getting closer to God each time. Whatever this new plan turned out to be, Polly and I knew God wasn't going to like us breaking into His house, and I didn't much think we'd see any miracles.

Delores had been wanting a sister all of her life. That was the reason she was jealous of me. It seemed like my mama was always expecting a baby. She had me, then 'Becca, then Arlene, and finally Carson junior. But Aunt Boo only had Delores. That was a little strange to me because anyone would surely want a nicer little girl than Delores. 'Course, I can't say I know of anyone that would want to be Delores's baby sister, so maybe the problem wasn't Aunt Boo after all. There probably wasn't one soul in heaven volunteering to take the job.

Every time one of her plans failed, Delores would sit on the front-porch steps with her chin in her hands and her elbows resting on her knees, just staring across the road at the chicken houses. She wouldn't talk or move for hours except to jiggle her foot up and down real fast against the brick steps. That's how I know Delores is planning something, and that always means trouble is coming. But no one else in our family seems to see this—they all think Delores is just perfect.

We were eating supper when she started in on this new plan, and as soon as she had gobbled all her food down, she gave me her orders.

"To the porch, quick," she told me.

I put off the meeting for as long as I could. I ate two helpings of rice and black-eyed peas, three pork chops, and a biscuit, but after that I ran out of room and excuses and had to leave the table. I found Delores sitting on the top step, leaning against the railing and tapping that foot of hers.

"We're doing something wrong, Sissy. You've got to ask your mama how people make babies."

"No way, Delores. You're crazy. You want a baby—you go ask her."

She answered me with a pinch, another one of those twisting, squeezing kinds on the soft skin under my arm.

"Okay, okay, but you have to come too," was the only answer I could give her then.

We found Mama sitting on the swing out in the backyard, reading a letter from my daddy. It's been a long time since he was last home, and Mama sits out there a lot. She says the noise of the crickets and the whippoorwills makes sweet music. I like to sit out there too, listening like her. But there's another sound I like even better than the birds and crickets. It's the sound of my mama's heart beating against my head when I lean against her, watching the night clouds skittering across the moon, and the stars winking on and off. It's hard not to fall asleep wrapped up in all that love. I always want that feeling to last a long, long time. Granny says being close like that is a good thing, that everybody needs "pettin' up sometimes, 'specially young girls." But Delores never thinks about those kinds of feelings. She rushed right out there and plopped down on the ground in front of Mama, dragging me by the shirt and pulling me down beside her. The night air felt cool and soft, and I watched Mama sitting there using one foot to push herself back and forth on the swing. She was humming low, but I couldn't catch the tune because Delores kept clearing her throat to signal me to get on with the questions.

"Uh, Mama?" I started out.

"Mmm?"

"Mama—Delores wants me to ask you how to make her mama have a baby sister for her."

Delores curled her lips back at me and poked my side, her finger sinking deep into the space between my ribs. She hates it when I use her name so people can know I'm not the one asking the questions.

Mama sat straight up and crossed her legs and arms, which made the swing jerk back two times and then stop. She put her hand up over her mouth like she always does when I surprise her with questions. It's like she's trying to stop the words from coming out before she has a chance to think about them. That's a rule in my family—thinking before you talk. Mama says it doesn't take but a second or two to keep from saying things you might regret, but this time her hand stayed up longer than usual.

"Well, umm, why don't you just ask your mama, Delores? You know, havin' a baby is a personal matter, and you really should have a private talk with her rather than with me. I'm sure she'd like to know that you're curious about it."

"Aunt Boo won't talk about it, Mama. She keeps tellin' Delores that it's in God's hands. I keep tellin' Delores to listen to her mama, but she thinks God needs a little help. Besides, it'll be a while before Delores goes back home, and she needs to know tonight."

Mama's hand floated back up to her mouth, and her feet made the swing jerk again. I watched her tapping her fingers against her lips and wondered what the words were that she didn't want to say.

Soon the crickets hushed, and the nighttime quiet got louder and louder, but for once Delores didn't fidget around. She sat quiet and waiting, like me. Finally Mama stood up and walked behind the swing. Her finger poked in and out of the chain, rubbing the inside of each of the silver links. Then she pulled a tissue from her pocket, wet it with her tongue, and scrubbed at the black smears the chain had made on her finger.

"Well, now, let me see," she said, and her hand rose to her mouth again.

"Makin' babies is a very natural thing, girls. It's as natural as—as farmin'—you know, like Big Daddy. You see, the farmer and the land are like the husband and the wife. They work together to raise a crop—which is, oh, you know, like the baby. The seeds have to be planted in the land, and then the farmer fertilizes them, and pretty soon, why, you have a baby—I mean a crop. You see?"

I didn't, but Mama looked so wishful I couldn't let her down.

"Uh, yes, m'am. I think we do, Mama."

"Oh, good. Good. Yes, well, you two run along now," she said, and sat down on the swing again.

The story didn't make any sense to me, but Delores said she had heard that women have the baby seeds inside of them, so all we needed was to find the right fertilizer. She thought that since vitamins and fresh vegetables helped people grow strong, they must be the fertilizer for babies too. So we raided Granny's garden for the freshest vegetables, and Delores took our Saturday movie money and bought a bottle of vitamins from the drugstore. There were a hundred pills in that bottle, as red and hard as dried kidney beans. Delores cracked them up with Granny's nutcracker and pounded them with the meat mallet until nothing but a sandy-feeling red powder was left. She hid the powder in a brown bag in her dresser. Then she pretended to be homesick and called Aunt Boo on the phone to ask her to please come down and stay with us a while. Aunt Boo did what Delores wanted. She stayed for a week, and every day before supper Delores would stir some of the vitamins into the pots of vegetables that are always simmering in Granny's kitchen.

At supper time, when Aunt Boo would start to help her plate from the stove, Delores would break in line to snatch the plate from her hand. Then that fake syrupy voice of hers would say, "Here, Mama, let me fix your supper. You go sit down. I'll bring it right over."

One night when Granny's friend Miss Viola was eating over at our house, the creamed corn was passed around, and Miss Viola asked Granny why it looked so pink.

"I just don't know, Viola, dear. It's the funniest thing; it was perfectly yellow when I put it on earlier today. It must be one of those new strains Big Daddy is tryin' out. It tastes a little sour, but a pinch of sugar takes care of that. I do hope you'll try some."

"Why of course I will, 'Melia, honey. It must be good; Boo over there has a plateful!" Miss Viola said as she smiled over at Aunt Boo.

Delores had piled so much corn on the plate that it was oozing over the edge onto Granny's good tablecloth. Big Daddy winked at me and said Aunt Boo must have plowed ten acres behind a mule if she was that hungry. But Aunt Boo ignored his joke and turned to talk to Miss Viola.

"Delores is tryin' very hard to be helpful, Miss Viola. Why, she's just turnin' into the most thoughtful daughter you can imagine! It's so important to reward girls for their efforts, don't you think?"

"Certainly, by all means. Reward efforts, indeed." Miss Viola slid her eyes over toward me and winked. No one ever fooled her, not even Delores. Teaching dancing lessons to us had made Miss Viola a wise woman, but poor Aunt Boo still had not caught on to the real picture.

Not too long after that, bridge night came around, and all the ladies were getting together at Granny's. Aunt Boo came down to visit again, and Mama asked Delores and me to help serve the refreshments. I stacked the cheese biscuits in a giant pyramid on the silver tray, and Delores poured Granny's homemade peach brandy into the glasses.

"Okay, they're ready," I said, lifting the tray and turning toward Delores so we could go in together. "Delores, what are you doin'? Granny'd kill you if she saw you stickin' your finger down in all those glasses!"

"Shut up, Sissy! Be quiet. I was stirring in some of the fertilizer, and I forgot which glass I was going to give to Mama, so I had to mix it in all of them."

"D-e-l-o-r-e-s!" I knew we were going to have trouble now. Granny prided herself on making the sweetest peach brandy around; those vitamins were sure to turn it sour.

Delores gave me a shove that sent my beautiful pyramid of biscuits tumbling to the floor, and Granny walked in right then.

"Sissy, what in the world! Lord, you've gone and ruined the biscuits. Go on, get out of the way now.

I'll have to serve somethin' else. Delores, you go on in, sweetie, and serve the brandy to the ladies, then come back and take in some of these little nuts and things. That'll hold 'em for a while."

Delores tossed her head back, swinging her ponytail in my face, and prissed on up to the living room. I went outside to the swing, but it wasn't long before Delores found me.

"Come on, Sissy. Let's go listen in."

About the only time I like having Delores around is when the grown-ups get together. She can always find a way to hide us out close enough to listen in on their talk. Most of what we know about the people in our town, we learned this way. Granny says eavesdropping is rude and always leads to trouble one way or another. 'Course, I found out later that she was right about the trouble part, but that night, scrunched down beside the hydrangea bush under the living-room window, her warnings weren't real.

Delores and I squatted there in the dirt eating two of the biscuits I had picked up on my way out of the kitchen. Granny would have fussed, because any food that touches the floor in her house gets thrown to the pigs, but I didn't see any sense in giving those biscuits to them. I just rubbed the biscuits across the front of my shirt and then blew on them, so they were perfectly good. Even Delores, as prissy as she tries to be sometimes, didn't complain. For a while her company wasn't so bad. The night was cool, and a breeze kept the mosquitoes away while we sat nibbling at the little chunks of cheese buried in the biscuits and listening to the talk through the open window.

Pretty soon, though, Granny's warnings would start coming true. Big Daddy says Granny's peach brandy could liven up the dead, and it sure went to work on those ladies in the living room that night. Somebody said something about seeing Mary Jo kissing Sam Plumber right on Main Street, and how that was for sure going to lead to news. Then Mrs. Branson, I could tell it was her because of her voice—she's a Yankee—she said, "That's right, we all know what kissing can do. Just look at me!"

"That must have been some kiss, Celia. It's twins this time, isn't it?" Mama's voice sounded a little louder than usual.

"Well you ought to know, Zan. You must like kissing a whole lot—look at all the children you have. What about you, Boo?"

"Who, me? Why, Celia, you know I don't like kissing—don't like it one little bit!" When the ladies heard that, the whole room filled up with laughs.

"Now listen, that's enough of that kind of talking. Y'all are letting this conversation get out of hand. It's dirty, just plain common and dirty! We're here to play CARDS, ladies." Aunt Boo's voice sounded strong and sure, but I could hear a little laugh underneath it.

There was so much hooting then, I thought the house would shake for sure. I looked over at Delores, thinking she'd be laughing too, but she was staring all glassy-eyed off into the night, and her left foot was tapping away next to mine.

"So that's how it's done," she whispered. "The fertilizer is in the kisses!"

"Yeah, well how does it work, Miss Smartypants?" I sneered at her.

"I'm not real sure. But remember when Mama caught us in that spit fight that time, and she fussed so long about spreading germs through spit? Then just now she said kissing was dirty. That's got to be it—if you kiss, you must get spit on the other person, and spit is dirty, so she doesn't like it. Gosh, Sissy, my mama's never going to give me a baby sister."

Delores's foot tapped faster, but after a while it stopped without any warning, and she crawled away, leaving me alone under the window. I wasn't sure that Delores had understood what her mama said about the kissing stuff, but I did know one thing. No way was I going to collect spit for her. All I could think of was the jars of black slimy stuff that the old men kept under their chairs when they sat and talked in front of the feed store. If that was her next idea, she would just have to do it on her own, or else come up with another plan.

And that's just what she did. At six o'clock the next morning Delores snatched the pillow from under my head and plopped a dripping cold wash-cloth down on my face.

"Get up," she whispered. "We've got to go to the church."

"Church? Why? We can't go to church, it's locked up."

Her breath was hot on my face when she leaned close, and those eyes of hers were hard and glassy again, like doll eyes, when she hissed into my ear, "I'll tell your mama about the rabbit tobacco and the nasty jokes you told last week."

I don't know why God gave me a cousin like Delores, and I don't know how she finds out everything. Polly and I had picked some rabbit to-bacco, and I took some of Big Daddy's rolling papers from his box on the dresser. We hid behind the old schoolhouse, smoking and telling every bad joke we could. We hadn't invited Delores, but she must have followed us, because she knew it all. I made up my mind right then to be more careful around her, but that didn't help Polly and me this time. We didn't have a choice except to follow Delores to the church, and that's when all of Granny's warnings came true. And the real trouble began.

It seemed like Polly and I had been on our knees for hours, but Delores was still going strong. She had been reading Bible verses from the pulpit, but then she stopped and tapped her foot against the carpet for a while. I peeked out from underneath my eyelids and watched as she moved candles up to the communion table. When she had twelve of them circling the crucifix, Delores disappeared into the reverend's office at the back of the church and then came out wearing his long white robe.

Without the lights on, the sanctuary was dark and cool like those caves over on Pit Road that the highway men left when they dug out the clay. But it didn't stay dark for long. Delores marched slowly up the aisle with her arms folded across her stomach and her hands hiding inside those giant robe sleeves. When she reached the altar, her hands slid out of the sleeves and with a lot of waving around, Delores lit the candles, making the brass of the crucifix sparkle with red, yellow, and gold lights. She walked up to stand behind the table with her arms spread wide out to the side, and the candles made her shadow look like a big black bird-creature against the wall. The quiet in the church turned spooky.

"Delores, what are you doin'?"

"We're going to pray for my miracle baby. What we need is a clean conception."

"A clean what?"

"A clean conception. I figured it all out. Mama thinks kissing is dirty, so if I'm going to get a baby sister, it's got to be a clean conception—you know, like Mary. The Immaculate Conception."

"Delores, that's not what it means," Polly said.

"It is too. I looked it up in the dictionary. *Immaculate* means perfectly clean."

"I'm not believin' this, Delores. You are s-o-o-o stupid!" I was really getting tired of all this baby business.

"Sissy, you are going to do this with me—you and Polly—or I swear I'll make you sorry. Now get over there and play that piano. Polly, you pray."

Polly and I had already had so much trouble with our mamas on account of Delores that there just wasn't anything to do but play and pray.

I fumbled around with a hymn, and Polly prayed just loud enough for Delores to hear her, but not clear enough for her to know what she was saying. Delores stretched her arms out again, closed her eyes, and then flung her head back just like those visiting tent preachers do.

"Oh, God and Jesus, send down your Holy Ghost to fertilize my mama. She's a good, clean woman like Mary. Give her a baby, please!"

I have to say, Delores had the praying part down almost perfectly. I'd never seen or heard much better. While her voice got louder, her arms rose up, up over her head, and then she started moaning just like the real thing. Polly and I couldn't help but stop the praying and playing to watch the show she was putting on.

"Oh, God and Jesus, give us a sign that you can hear our prayers!"

Delores began to twirl her body around and around the communion table. The reverend's white robe swished and swirled, and the big sleeves floated in the air like giant, soft angel wings. Delores moaned some more and twirled faster and faster, churning up the air inside the church, and that's when God sent us the sign Delores had prayed for.

The reverend's robe sleeves burst into flames.
Delores screamed and ripped the reverend's robe
right off her body. She backed into the communion
table, crashing it to the floor and sending all those
candles rolling and spreading flames everywhere.
Polly and I started stomping on them as fast as we
could, but Delores ran toward the door crying and
screaming at the top of her voice. And that's when
the trouble arrived. The reverend's voice blasted
out above Delores's screams and filled the whole
sanctuary.

"What in heaven's name is going on here?" he
shouted. He ran up the aisle, pushing past Delores,
and stood shaking in front of the altar where Polly
and I stood. I had never heard the reverend raise his
voice like that, never seen his face so red—not even
during revival.

Not one of us could answer. Candle wax and
burn holes spotted the red altar carpet. The crucifix
lay on the floor, its base broken off, and the reverend's white robe was singed black and smeared
with our sooty footprints. He bent over and lifted it
carefully between two fingers and then dropped it
back down onto the ruined carpet.

Delores sank like the sun behind the reverend's

back as he glared at Polly and me. We could see her glassy eyes squinting at us from behind his elbow, and her foot was already tapping away. She was thinking all right, but this was one time I wasn't going to take the blame for her. She could tell the whole world about the tobacco and bad jokes. Nothing was going to top the trouble we were in now.

"Uh, Reverend. Uh, you see, um, Delores was tryin' to have an Immaculate Conception."

"A what?"

"You know. Like Mary. Just ask Delores. She knows all about it."

The reverend's face looked as if it might explode. He stood with his fists all knotted up into hard balls, and his arms looked stiff, like two boards. His cheeks puffed out and his face turned even redder than the carpet. In my mind I could see smoke blowing out of his ears like in the cartoons when the characters get so mad, but slowly he stretched out his fingers, then he rubbed one hand across the front of his shirt a few times and used his other hand to wipe across his face, pulling his eyes, cheeks, and mouth down, making him look like some sad kind of clown. His hand hung over his mouth for a few seconds, like he had heard Mama's rule about thinking before you speak. We never heard the words he stopped himself from saying, just his quiet, shaky voice when he turned to leave and said, "Follow me, please."

'Course, he headed straight to Granny's house. Delores skipped right up beside him, crying and talking, and waving her arms all around trying to explain things. Polly and I couldn't help laughing at the way she looked, that ponytail jiggling all around, and those long legs of hers bowing and stretching to keep up with the reverend's steps.

The whole story had to be told three times, once to Granny and Mama, then to Polly's mom, and finally to Aunt Boo when she came to Granny's after Delores called her crying. It was a mess for sure. Delores cried so much she broke out in hives, and Aunt Boo took her back home to the city. Polly and I spent the next day scrubbing the church walls and scraping wax from the communion table. The new carpet was installed a week later, and the crucifix was fixed. The reverend got a brand-new white robe, and the deacons started a children's Bible study class on the meanings of Bible words. The congregation members all got apology notes from Delores, but Polly and I never did, naturally.

And there was never any news from Aunt Boo

about a new baby either, but I think I've figured out why. I heard the grown-ups talking about somebody being a bad seed, and from what I can work out in my mind, Delores must be one of them. So it makes good sense that Aunt Boo wouldn't want to risk having another baby. Poor Delores will be so disappointed when she hears that.

High-Stepping

It was good to be out on the dock in the dark coldness of the early morning. Big Daddy and Tyrus stood near the bank, slurping coffee and watching the tide creep out to the middle of the inlet. I stood farther down, slurping my coffee in time with them and breathing in the hot steam that rose from the heavy white mug up into the cold air, just like the fog rising off the warm water on those first frosty mornings of fall. I was proud to be drinking coffee with them, but I knew Granny wouldn't have approved.

"Coffee stunts your growth," she always warned, and since I'm only eleven, she says I've still got a lot of growing to do.

But Big Daddy says, "A few cups here and there

won't make no nevermind." So we both promised not to tell Granny anything about it. I know I can trust him too. Big Daddy's real good at three things: telling stories, keeping secrets, and playing jokes on people.

That's why I was along for the hunting trip today. Ever since Big Daddy quit farming the land at the point, he and Tyrus had been taking Yankee hunters down there on the weekends during hunting season. Most of the time the trips were serious business, but every year a group of Yankees would come down who didn't know anything about duck hunting in the marshes, and that's when Big Daddy and Tyrus had all the fun. 'Course, they always sent the Yankees home tired, happy, and with what Tyrus called "a new 'preciation for Southern hospitality," but that didn't stop them from playing a few tricks on 'em. I had heard all the stories about breaking in the visitors, but this was the first time I would see it for myself. Big Daddy and Tyrus don't let just anybody in on their pranks, and I was prouder than anything to be going along.

"How long dey stayin', Mr. Bill?"

"Just the weekend, Tyrus. We'll let 'em hunt today and fish tomorrow if the weather's right. You switched those gun shells?"

I could just make out Tyrus's gray head nodding and then his white teeth sparkled from inside that crooked grin of his. "Reckon we'll have to break 'em in fast den. Me and Sissy'll take 'em over to de blinds and den come back and check de traps. Dey'll be plenty hungry by lunch and wantin' somethin' hot fer sho'."

Big Daddy did that deep growling laugh of his, and a cold tickling ran up my spine.

The three Yankee men stomped out to the dock, and Tyrus led us down to the marsh edge. The reeds grew knee-high, and the great spread of rich, black pluff-mud stretched across the inlet to two small islands about half a mile away. Jagged clumps of oyster shells dotted the naked marsh bottom and then disappeared beneath the skinny ribbon of water left by the low tide. Tyrus let his eyes run over the dark ground and then stepped right out into the pluff. Standing straight and tall, he pointed his crooked nub of a finger east toward the two islands. I loved looking at Tyrus's nub. He lost that finger in a boat-rigging accident when he was little, and the skin had grown back thick and coiled like buoy ropes, all white-speckled across the dark skin on his knucklebone.

"Dat dere's where we's going, and we's best get

movin' so's y'all can get hunkered down afore dem mallards start flyin'. Dey'll be risin' early 'cause of last night's frost."

He jerked the strings of his hood tight under his chin and shouldered the big cloth sack that bulged with mysterious lumps. I kept to his tracks just like he had taught me, looking for those almost-hidden mounds of oyster shells sealed over and packed hard with mud that would give me a sure way through the soupy pluff. Behind us the Yankees marched fast through the reeds. They talked a lot, especially Mr. Booker. He had a loud, whining voice and didn't seem to pay attention to what anybody else said. The three of them all stepped flat-footed right into the marsh, and the slurpy, sucking marsh sounds grew louder as the men struggled to keep up with Tyrus and me. We had hardly got started good when out of the dark came, "Ah, damn it. I lost my boot!" The words were followed by a muffled wet thud and then another loud string of cussing. From over by the dock we heard Big Daddy's laugh, and we knew without seeing that he was watching as one by one the men lost their boots to the sucking mud and tumbled facedown into the sticky wetness of the marsh.

Tyrus and I turned around, and when he started back toward the Yankees, he whispered to me, "Yep,

Sissy. Jus' like de others. Dey don' know nothin' 'bout marshes and mud. Don't you laugh now, girl."

The three men were wallowing on their hands and knees in the shallow water. When they struggled to stand up, their boots stuck tight and their feet came out of them. Their socks, filled up with the mud and water, slid down and flapped around their toes like beagle ears, leaving six scaly white heels shining in the gray light.

Mr. Booker was the worst. He was wet front and back, and he lost his cap and one of his gloves somewhere in the thick reeds. Tyrus dug around in his sack and pulled out towels to hand the men. After slinging the soggy socks back toward the bank, the Yankees squirmed their cold bare feet down into the mud-lined boots, and we started out again.

It took a while to get them settled in the duck blinds and the sky was just streaked with light when Tyrus handed each of the men a pint bottle labeled "Rebel Yell." The Yankees hooted at the name, and Tyrus and I laughed too, but not because of that. Tyrus kept those bottles filled with his own bootleg—"powerful enough to curl yo' hair," he bragged. The Yankees didn't know any better, and after a few slugs they didn't care. The only things left for Tyrus and me to do were to stash his sack behind another duck blind and warn the hunters not to shoot each other. They didn't know that there wasn't any shot in the shells. Then we crossed back over the marsh toward home, leaving the Yankees, the Rebel Yell, and the ducks to the "Lord's luck" as Tyrus said.

Off and on during the morning we saw the black *V*'s flying overhead and heard the shotguns crack. Later we heard the cracks, but saw no ducks, so by midmorning after the fish lines and crab traps were baited for the afternoon, Tyrus and I started back to the island.

We uncovered the stashed sack, and at the first blind, we found Mr. Booker stretched out on his back with his gun barrel tucked under his chin. A line of sand fiddlers skittered across his chest and up his arm, and an empty bottle of Rebel Yell was stuck neck-down into the marsh mud.

"Wonder where he put de cap?" Tyrus asked as he stuck the empty bottle in his sack and nudged Mr. Booker with the toe of his boot. We moved on and found the other two men snoring in the second blind, and after Tyrus woke them, he opened up the mouth of his sack and hauled out a large green-headed drake that was missing a foot.

"Looks like y'all had a good mornin' fer sho',"
he laughed. "I counts seven all told—one drake and
six hens."

The Yankees looked a little confused, but they
smiled and slapped each other on the back and then
stumbled around collecting their guns. I caught Mr.
Booker looking down into the sack like maybe he
wanted to count those ducks himself, but Tyrus
grabbed it up quick and headed toward the inlet.

"Now gent'men—afore we starts back, y'all best
knows dat de goin' can be trickier than de comin'.
De tide is risin' and ya gotta walk careful so's you
don' fall in some of dem deep holes out dere. Jus'
you walks in a straight line right behind me, and
walks jus' like I walk—ya heah?"

He winked at me as he stepped up in front of the
tottering men. "Y'all ready now?"

The Yankees shouldered their guns, and I took
my place behind them and a little to the left so I
could get a good look.

"Let's go—jus' like me now. Y'all walks jus' like
me."

Tyrus pulled his knee high up toward his chin,
then stretched his long leg straight out in front of
his body, flattened his foot and brought it down in
the rising creek water. With each stretch of his leg

his body arched backward, and as his boot settled in the water, his head and neck lurched forward.

"We calls dis de crane walk, boys, 'cause high-steppin' is de onliest way to get through pluff-mud fast and dry."

The Yankees, drunk as they were, tried hard to copy Tyrus's every move, but not knowing what to look for before stepping, each rising leg would send them tumbling facedown into the mud. When they bent their bodies forward or backward trying to copy Tyrus, down they'd go again, and the slurping, sucking sounds were soon drowned out by grunts and curses. We staggered on across the pluff; Tyrus high-stepping his way from mound to mound, the Yankees wallowing and rolling through the pluff, and me holding my sides to keep from laughing. Halfway home we heard the dinner bell clanging, and Tyrus and I knew Big Daddy was watching again and slapping his knees at the sight of the Yankees high-stepping across that marsh.

The Yankees, all mud-coated and shivering from the cold, held up the day's kill and grinned at Big Daddy while he snapped four pictures with his camera. Then the visitors staggered up toward the house and disappeared into the outside showers. We were just going into the storage shed when we heard the first string of curse words coming from the cold showers.

Big Daddy's shoulders shook up and down, and he looked over sideways toward me and Tyrus. "Tyrus, I s'pose you forgot to warn 'em 'bout the hot water, huh?"

"Dat I did, Mr. Bill. Dat I did," Tyrus chuckled.

We tossed the ducks into the freezer and washed the Rebel Yell bottles. Tyrus unloaded the blank shells from the guns, then cleaned them, before we headed down to the bait store. The local men would want to know about the hunting, he said.

I love to listen to Tyrus's stories. He took his time telling all about those Yankees, and the old men chuckled and slapped their knees. Old Man Thomas walked behind the counter and pointed at a row of old pictures mounted with thumbtacks to the corkboard.

"Did de ducks look just like these, Tyrus?" he asked.

"Yessir, dey sho' did—jus' like 'em," Tyrus laughed back at him.

I scrambled up on the stool to get a good look and sure enough, there they were. A row of five pictures; three men in each one, mud-coated, bare-footed, and proudly displaying six hens and a large drake with only one foot.

At supper Big Daddy and Tyrus explained to the Yankees about how we were going to seine for shrimp and do some line fishing for crabs the next day. Mr. Booker didn't look too happy about going out in the pluff again, but after the Rebel Yell bottles were passed around a few times, he livened up quite a bit. When the bottles were empty, the talk got louder, and Big Daddy and Tyrus just sat there listening and nodding, while the Yankees bragged about the morning's hunt. Then somebody mentioned the pluff-mud, and Mr. Booker leaned across the arm of his chair with one arm dragging on the floor and the other one waving up in the air. His eyes were red and droopy, and they rolled around the room trying to find something he could fasten them on to, but he finally settled for just aiming his voice over toward where Tyrus was sitting.

"Tell me, Tyrus—just what is the secret to getting across that stinking pluff-stuff? I walked just like you said, but I got wetter 'n hell and you didn't."

Tyrus reared back in his chair until the front legs came up off the floor and his gray head rested against the wall behind him. He took his pipe and tapped it three times against his palm and then packed it tight with fresh tobacco. He sucked real deep for several seconds while he held the match to the bowl. All three of those Yankees leaned toward him, and then Tyrus cut his eyes at me and Big Daddy and grinned that slow, big smile. His head dropped down to rest on his chest for just a minute, as if he was thinking real hard before he answered. Then he stood up, stretched his arms way up high in the air, and yawned loud. The three of us got to the back door before Tyrus turned around to answer Mr. Booker.

"Why, gent'men," he grinned, "dere ain't no se-cret—it's jus' common sense. To keep from sinkin' in de pluff, ya gots to put all yo weight on de leg what's up in de air."

Black Patent-Leather, High-Heeled Shoes

They sat in the front window at Mr. Jim's Shoe Shop. The afternoon sun streaked across the red carpet and then bounced off the glassy toes. Onyx Beauties the sign said. Mr. Jim names all of his shoes. They were beauties too. I just knew they were smooth as glass. Every Saturday I walked by that window making sure they were still there.

What I wanted most that spring was that pair of black patent-leather, high-heeled shoes. Black patent-leather, high-heeled shoes—the words had a special sound to them, like a cymbal tinkling out the beat at the beginning of a song. I tapped it out down the cracked sidewalks in town, down Granny's long hall, even with my fork against my plate at supper every night. Black patent-leather, high-heeled shoes, yeah, that's what I wanted most in all the world.

But mama had said, "NO." She said no in that hard final voice she uses when she means "Sissy, you've gone over the line." There's never any way around that "NO"—it stretches out to cut off any of my usual "But, Mamas." It's not like the slurry "NO" that means "Well, maybe," not even like the hurried-up "NO" that tells you to come back later and ask again. This one means just plain "NO!"

That kind of "NO" is usually the end of things, but Granny heard my talk with Mama and she followed me out to the yard, catching the screen door I meant to slam hard.

"Sissy, come here, girl. Let's talk about these shoes a minute. Just why do you need a new pair of shoes?"

"Black patent-leather, high-heeled shoes, Granny! They're the only kind I want. The junior high school is havin' a dance for all of us sixth graders moving up next year, and I've just got to have 'em. I'll die if I have to go to that dance lookin' like some old baby!"

I didn't tell her about Larry. He was what I wanted second best that spring. Larry was the cutest boy in school. He was also grade president and a baseball star. I had known him forever; my family knew his well. We used to spend a lot of time together, but all of that ended when he went up to junior high. He was so popular, and all the girls had crushes on him. Those shoes could be my big chance to get Larry's attention and show him I wasn't a baby anymore. But I couldn't tell Granny all of that.

"Well, I think I understand, Sissy. Tell you what, you just let me think on this a while." Granny sat down in the porch rocker, and I listened to the squeak and creak music it made while she thought about how to get around that "No" of Mama's.

"It could be, I could convince your mama to let you get the shoes if you are willin' to pay for them. Are you willin' to work to get those shoes?"

"I will, Granny, I will. Just tell me what you want me to do. I'll do anythin'."

"When is this dance now?"

"It's in early May, right before school lets out, Granny."

"Mmmmm, this just might work. And you say you'll do anythin' to get those shoes?"

"Yes, m'am—anythin'."

I didn't really mean *anything*, but I never thought my own granny would hold me to that word and trick me like she did.

"Well now. I know I'll be needin' some help with the baby chicks when they come in. You could help me raise them, you know, tend to the mash and the water, help me keep the lanterns burnin'. It will take about six weeks to raise the biddies up big enough to put out in the yard, and that dance of yours will come right after that, so I think we can work this out—if you're willin' to do some work."

"Oh, no, not the chickens, Granny. You know I hate those chickens. I'll do anythin' else you want me to do, but please don't make me tend to those chickens."

"Now, Sissy. If you want somethin' bad enough, you've got to be willin' to do what it takes to get it. You need to learn about those chickens anyway. So this is the deal. I'll talk to your mama, you'll help me with the chicks, and then you can buy those new shoes of yours."

Those new shoes of mine—black patent-leather, high-heeled shoes, I said to myself.

I pretended to be asleep in the glider that afternoon while I listened to Granny talk to Mama about her deal. Mama kept saying things like, "She's too young. She'll break her neck. What will people say?"

And Granny'd answer back, "She's growin' up, Zan. We can get those cute little one-inch heels. People can see she's just in those caught-in-the-middle years. Don't you remember what it was like?"

"Yes, I do remember," Mama said softly. "They are mixed-up and changin' years, and I don't want Sissy rushin' headlong into them. There's plenty of time yet for some things."

It was hard to picture Mama being my age, wanting the same things I want now. I never would have thought she knew so much. But one thing she didn't know about was how I felt about Larry, and that made all the difference. He was the real reason I had to have those shoes.

The talk went on a little longer, but finally Mama said, "All right. If she works for them, she can have them, but that's between you and Sissy. I don't have time to worry about her keepin' her part of the bargain."

'Course, I was glad Mama had given in, but I still had to think a while about Granny's deal. Messing with those chickens was a dirty job. There's nothing good about 'em except the way they taste all fried up gold and crispy.

But in the end I decided to do it. I thought maybe Granny would feel sorry for me and just get me the shoes and forget the deal after a time, but she didn't.

The boxes arrived one afternoon.

"Sissy, our chicks are heah!" Granny called. "Run out and put these lightbulbs in and fill the kerosene lamps. Oh, and fill those water jars full and set out some of that mash too."

The chicken yard sits way at the back of the lot. There are a couple of oak trees inside the fence, but the rest of the yard is just dirt and henhouses. Big Daddy built the houses from old boards, and every year Granny puts fresh hay in each of the boxes for the laying hens. Chicken snakes love those boxes. I don't like collecting eggs because of them. They sneak under the hay and just when your hand reaches in to curl around a big brown egg, those snakes pop up their heads and hiss at you. Big Daddy says chicken snakes won't hurt you, but I think they could surely scare a person to death.

Big Daddy built the new coop for the chicks outside the chicken yard. It stood about three feet off the ground, and one side could be lifted all the way up. There were two shelves inside; the bottom shelf held two kerosene lamps that would burn all the time to keep the chicks from freezing, and the top shelf was a slide-out tray that would catch the droppings through the wire cage the chicks would be raised in. Above this were two electric sockets for lightbulbs that would give off more heat. The top of the coop lifted up too, so you could put the chicks in and take them out when you needed, but you weren't supposed to lift it just to look inside. The heat would get out, and the chicks would die. There were two peepholes in the wooden sides to look through to check on them.

I left to do what Granny had asked. I filled the lanterns, and then wiped off the kerosene that had splashed on the sides, turned the wicks up just enough to give low flames, lit them, and then snapped the glass globe down in place. It wouldn't take long to heat up the coop, but I flipped the lightbulbs on too, just in case. Granny had bought new water jars, and I loved the slick feel of the glass as it curved up to form the saucers where the water would stand when the jars were filled and turned upside down. Those parts of caring for the chicks weren't so bad. It was the droppings tray I hated.

"Here we are, little chickies," Granny crooned over the boxes as she brought them out. She cut the wires that held the boxes shut and lifted the lids away. The smell whooshed up smack in my face.

"Pheww!" I gasped, and choked.

Baby chicks were everywhere. They climbed over each other, cheeping and pecking at everything— tiny yellow fluff balls on skinny stick legs.

"Carefully now, Sissy. Lift one at a time, and ease 'em into the coop. I'll open it up."

My hands felt the soft feathers first—that wasn't bad at all, but then my fingers slid under and around the bottom of the chick to cradle it. The stick legs hung down between my fingers with the feet dangling and clawing at the air. Halfway to the coop, I felt it—the bad part. Green poop slid from between my fingers and plopped right on the toe of my tennis shoe. But I knew there wasn't any need to complain. That was only the first chick—there were one hundred and two in those boxes!

The chicks went right to work doing what chicks do best, eating and pooping. They walked through the mash, in the water saucers, and poop piled up everywhere they walked, dripping down through the screen and into the tray. Granny's new coop was a mess already!

The unpacking was just the beginning of the work. The water had to be changed four times a day, and the saucers scrubbed clean. I didn't like to feel the slick curves anymore. The chicks ate all the time, so I was forever scooping fresh mash, which just meant I had to clean the poop tray again. I used the water hose and Granny's old wire scrub-brush for that. It has a long handle, and if I didn't squirt the water too hard and too close to the tray, none of the poop splashed on me, but Mama made me leave my tennis shoes outside by the door anyway.

"There's no savin' those," she said. I worried that she'd make me use my money to buy new tennis shoes, but she never said, and so I kept on dreaming about those black patent-leather, high-heeled shoes.

We tended the chicks for two weeks before the weather turned. Big Daddy says the weather always turns cold again right before Easter, "'cause God wants to make sure we 'preciate the spring."

Then one morning, just like he had said, the weather changed.

"Sissy, Sissy girl, get up quick. I need your help." Granny tugged at the quilt bundled around me.

"There's been a big frost. Get your coat. We've got to check the chicks!"

I grumbled all the way to my tennis shoes by the door, but outside, the cold air slapped my face and chased the sleep from my eyes. The new spring grass was covered by a layer of pearly frost that sparkled when Granny's flashlight swept across it. I pulled my jacket close and crunched over to the coop behind the dancing light.

I peeped through the hole in the side of the coop. The lights were burning, and the chicks looked like a big yellow pillow spread across the cage. They huddled against and under each other, peeping soft and low. Everything looked okay, until Granny lifted the side of the coop so she could turn up the lanterns. She pushed the soft fuzzy bodies to one side and there below them was a layer of stiff, matted feathers and straight legs with feet that curled into tight, hard balls.

"Oh, poor little chickies," Granny sighed. She lit an extra lantern and turned up the wick on the other two.

"Best to leave 'em for now, Sissy. Can't tell much in the dark. We've probably lost a good many."

I left my shoes by the door and spent the rest of the night huddling under my quilt. I felt sorry for the chicks, but I was more worried about my shoes, my black patent-leather, high-heeled shoes. I thought if all the chicks died, there would be no money to buy them.

"Coldest night on record for this time of year," Big Daddy reported at breakfast.

But before I left for school, the sun burned off the frost, and Granny sent me out to check the chicks again. There was a lot of loud peeping from the coop.

"Always hungry," I grumbled, and poured the mash at one end of the coop. The chicks squabbled and clawed their way to the far side, not minding the stiff bodies they stepped on. I grabbed a basket and started lifting out the dead bodies. With two fingers I pinched the legs and pulled the dead ones out, dropping them into the basket. The feathers were pasted flat against their sides from the screen wire and where the other chicks had nestled on top of them. They looked so pitiful and small, I did start to cry a little. All that mash must go straight in and then out, because there just wasn't any meat on those bodies.

I counted thirty-four dead chicks and lifted the basket to haul it to the backyard near the woods to bury them. Just as I was emptying the chicks into the hole, I heard someone walk by on the path that ran alongside our yard and through the woods. It was Larry. I had forgotten that he used the path to walk to the bus stop.

"Hey, Sissy!" he called out.

I couldn't believe my luck! There I was, toting dead chicks around and crying over them when Larry, of all people, came down that path. I pretended not to hear, but Larry jumped the low fence to come over to see what I was doing.

"The frost get 'em last night?" he asked.

I nodded my head, keeping my eyes on the bottom of that hole.

"How many did ya lose?" he tried again.

I shrugged my shoulders.

Larry stood there and watched as I thumped the last dead chick from the basket.

"Want me to help you cover 'em up?"

I shook my head no, and after a few seconds he cleared his throat.

"Well, guess I'll see ya around then," he said. I stood staring down into the hole until I was sure he had left. When I finally went to change my clothes for school, I realized that the bargain I had made with Granny wasn't working out quite the way I had planned.

But the next few weeks brought Easter and warmer weather. The chicks finally began to put on some weight. Granny never mentioned the dead biddies, and I never mentioned my shoes. But on Friday, the day before the dance, she woke me up early even though I didn't have to go to school.

"Sissy, go out and get the wagon. We need to move the chicks."

I didn't fuss. I'd do anything she asked. It was the day I'd get those new shoes of mine! I ran for the wagon.

Granny snapped the wooden side of the coop up and over the top, then reached in to slide one end of the wire cage out. The shifting caused the chicks to make a real fuss, and they cheeped and fluttered their tiny wings. The cage wasn't heavy, just big, and the chicks had grown to fill up most of the space. They pecked at my fingers curled inside the wire cage, not understanding that they were soon to be out of there. Granny and I put the cage on the wagon, and she pulled while I steadied it with one hand and pushed with the other all the way to the chicken yard.

"You can let 'em loose now, Sissy. Be careful they don't jump over the top of the cage and run away now. When you get them all inside, lock the gate, and then scrub down the cage and the coop with some lye soap."

I was careful, but I lost two chicks and had to chase them across the garden and around the house before I caught them. I watched them for a while just to make sure they settled in, but I didn't need to worry. Right away those chicks started pecking away at the dirt. The other chickens didn't seem to notice them, but the rooster was bossy as ever and chased a few of them around the yard before he settled down. By the time I finished the scrubbing, it was past dinnertime.

I left my tennis shoes by the door and went in to wash up, thinking Granny would want to leave for town soon. But Granny wasn't in the kitchen. She wasn't in the house at all. I found her note on the hall table:

Miss Viola is sick. I've gone to check on her.
Back tomorrow. Be good.

"Noooo," I screamed at the empty house. It wasn't fair. Miss Viola was always needing something. Why did Granny have to go? How could she forget about my new shoes? Maybe she wasn't going to stick to the deal, since so many of the chicks died. I stomped out of the house, barefooted, not caring about the sandspurs and rocks that covered the fields I ran across.

"Hey, Sissy, come 'ere," Polly called out as I raced passed her house. I didn't answer her. I didn't want to talk to anybody, not even to my best friend.

I spent the rest of the day walking, walking through the woods and down every dusty road I could find. I went to the creek and made a dam with rocks, but the current was too strong and the sand and rocks washed away. Nothing I did stopped the flow of the water, and nothing was going to stop tomorrow from coming. I wasn't going to have my black patent-leather, high-heeled shoes.

Supper was the same as always, except Granny wasn't there. No one noticed I didn't eat; no one noticed anything at all, and I went to bed early, knowing that there'd be no new shoes for the dance the next night.

"Sissy. Sissy, wake up. Got to feed the chickens and collect the eggs. Then after dinner we'll go to town for those new shoes of yours."

New shoes of mine? She said new shoes of mine! I sang the words over and over in my mind. I raced down the hall and out into the yard, not bothering to dress or put on my tennis shoes. I slung fist after fist of grain to the chickens and beat every board with a stick before reaching in to collect the eggs. I did all of this to the beat of black patent-leather, high-heeled shoes. Nothing was going to ruin my day today—not chickens, not snakes, and not even the poop that squished between my toes.

Careful is not the word to explain how well I washed that day. Hair, ears, underarms, and especially between my toes. I knew exactly what I was going to wear. I had pictured it for weeks—my black-and-white checked princess-waisted dress. By two o'clock I was dressed and ready for the dance, except for my shoes. Everything would be perfect when I got them.

The inside of Mr. Jim's Shoe Shop was cool and clean. I sat on the black vinyl chairs with one foot propped up on a footstool, the other on the floor while Mr. Jim measured carefully. He slid the metal scale snug against the side of my foot, pushing the rule down to rest on my big toe.

"Size five and one-half, wide. Must be goin' barefooted a lot, Miss Sissy," he said, winking at Granny. "Now which shoes do you want?"

"The, the . . ."—the words stuck and then blurted out too loud—"the black patent-leather, high-heeled shoes!"

"Oh," said Mr. Jim, settling back on his heels. He rubbed his chin with his four-fingered hand. Granny said he lost his thumb in the war, and any other time I would have stared at that hand, but I was worried he didn't have my shoe size.

"You mean my Onyx Beauties over there, Sissy? The ones with the little one-inch heels?" He didn't wait for my answer. He limped over to the window and held up those new shoes of mine.

"Yes," I whispered, and watched as the overhead lights danced across the slick leather. Slowly Mr. Jim brought them to me.

The hand with the missing thumb raised my foot, the other slipped the shoe, first over my toes, then with a light push, over and onto my heel. My breath stopped as my foot settled into the cushioned inside. Then the other shoe slid on, just like it was made for me, and suddenly I was standing for the first time in those new shoes of mine.

"Want me to wrap them up for you, Sissy?" Mr. Jim asked.

"Uh, no, sir. I think I'll wear them home, if it's all right with you." I smiled up at him. Granny handed me my chicken money, and I counted it out to Mr. Jim. There were two dollars left over.

On the way to the car I was careful to take small steps. The click of those heels on the sidewalk sent shivers up my spine. I felt that walking would never be the same again.

And it was different. I wobbled a little at first, trying to get my balance settled over the tiny heel. I walked for the rest of the afternoon—up and down Granny's long hall and across the front porch. I sat in the rocker and felt the cool, smooth leather, tracing every curve of those shoes with my fingers. I loved the feel of them, the smell of them. I loved me in them. I loved Granny for keeping the deal. I even loved those dumb chickens. The afternoon couldn't pass fast enough for me.

That night the gym was magic. From the door Polly and I could see the pink and blue balloons dangling from the ceiling on white streamers. A white cloth covered the two lunchroom tables at the far end, and plates of cookies and sandwiches lined them. Paper cups were stacked around a big glass bowl filled with punch. Music blared from the stage, and the seventh graders—no, they were eighth graders now—danced in center court. We hardly breathed, and then Larry came up behind us.

"Hey, y'all," he grinned.

My heart pounded, but I stuttered a "hey" back.

"Come on in," he said. "I'll show you 'round."

Polly punched me and I ribbed her, hoping Larry didn't see. He headed toward the gym doors, and

Polly and I rushed to walk in beside him. My new shoes and my plan were working just right!

But just as we stepped inside the double doors, a man's arm stretched out in front of us, blocking our way.

"Sorry, girls, you'll have to take off those shoes before you go in. They'll ruin the gym floor, you know."

I looked down at Polly's plain Mary Janes, then at my new patent-leather shoes, and finally at Larry's navy blue socks. In all our looking around, Polly and I had not noticed that everyone was wearing socks. We both blushed red, but Larry didn't seem to have heard the man, and he led us to the side of the room where a line of shoes spread across the floor.

"Stupid, stupid, stupid," I whispered more to myself than to Polly. "We don't even have any socks!"

We set our shoes down in the line with the others. Polly's Mary Janes were polished shiny white. They had been the "in thing" last year, but now, next to my Onyx Beauties, they looked like nothing at all.

"Hey, Sissy. Where'd you get those high-heeled shoes, from your mama?" The voice blasted through the open gym doors, from a group of boys standing there.

"Playin' dress-up tonight, Sissy?" blared another one.

Before I could stop her, Polly shouted back, "You shut up, Davey. Leave us alone."

The whole group laughed and took a running start, sliding toward us in their socks and right into the line of shoes by the wall. Polly stumbled and fell, and Davey grabbed up my new shoes and raced out of the building with the other boys following right behind.

I forgot that Larry was watching. All I could think of was getting my shoes back.

"Give me my shoes, Davey Sanders. Give 'em back or I'm gonna tell."

The laughs just got louder. My new shoes were tossed from one boy to another. Polly and I raced back and forth, grabbing at the air. Then from the corner of my eye I saw Larry and some of the other eighth graders watching it all. I didn't know which was worse, losing my shoes or having the eighth graders see Polly and me acting like silly little sixth graders.

Davey threw one last pitch, and one of my new

shoes went flying into the holly hedge.

"Stop that, boys. Stop that right now!" Coach Brunson pushed his way through the crowd that had gathered around us. Davey dropped my other shoe in the dirt, and the crowd went back inside. Polly and I were left alone.

The holly hedge was dark and thick. The pointed leaves stuck our hands as we reached in and out of the branches. Both of us were covered with scratches and pricks by the time we found my missing shoe.

Back inside under the gym lights, I worked hard not to cry. Those new shoes of mine were filthy, and the one that landed in the hedge looked ruined. The holly thorns had scratched the smooth shiny leather, and a sliver of stem stuck right out from the toe. I tucked them under Polly's Mary Janes in the line by the wall, hoping no one would see.

At least Polly had a lot of fun that night. She borrowed a pair of socks from a gym locker and danced every dance. I tried a couple of times, but my bare feet stuck to the waxed floor, making it hard to turn and slide, so when Larry asked me to dance, I said I wanted some punch instead. Without my shoes I didn't seem to belong at the dance, and without my socks I couldn't dance. I felt caught-in-the-middle for sure.

Granny found my shoes on my bed the next morning. I had fallen asleep rubbing the scratches and the hole. The next week she had Mr. Jim patch them up, and they didn't look bad at all. The leather was just as shiny as before, and the hole was only a tiny rough spot where he had filled it. You couldn't see it; only my finger could feel it. But I knew it was there, so I wore my Mary Janes to the sixth-grade graduation. Besides, they just seemed to fit better.

Summer started out hot. My chicks grew into chickens, and Granny had me collecting eggs every day. I was beating a stick against the side of one of the henhouses when Larry showed up one morning.

"Hey, Sissy. Whatcha doin'?"

I blushed, just like before in the gym, and I wondered if he remembered that night.

"I chase away the snakes like that too," he said when I didn't answer. "Say, you still play baseball?"

It was hard to answer him, but I finally mumbled a "Yeah, sometimes." Then I worried that maybe seventh-grade girls weren't supposed to play baseball.

"Well, some of us are gettin' up a game. You wanna play?"

I wasn't sure how to answer that either, but then Larry grinned and said, "Oh, come on. We need another player."

He helped me put the eggs away, and we started out side by side down the path through the woods, but Larry stopped all of a sudden and looked me right in the eye.

"I like those shoes of yours, Sissy."

At first I thought he was making fun of me and what had happened at the dance, but when I looked down at my feet, I saw that he was talking about my tennis shoes. I had forgotten to change them. There they were, dirty, with no strings, and speckled all over with chicken poop. Then my eyes slid over to Larry's shoes, and I just couldn't keep myself from laughing out loud.

"Yeah, and I like yours," I said, pointing down to his—they were speckled too.

Passion Puffs

"Blow on his neck.

"No, in his ear.

"Wait, wait, I know. Blow up his neck real slow, then hard and quick in his ear. That's how you do it."

"Jeez, Delores, can't you make up your mind?" I couldn't believe her, always giving orders and then changing them. This sex stuff was getting to be confusing and a lot like work. Ever since we turned thirteen, all she could talk about was how to get boys to like you, as if she knew all about it. Yeah, right.

I took the last chair in the line of rusty metal ones against the far wall. Just like every other Wednesday, two o'clock came and off we went in our pastel organdies, stiff crinolines scratching the tops of our sweaty thighs red and raw. Summer dancing lessons—what a treat.

"Now, boys and girls, we shall begin. Let's see, who will lead off today, hmmmm. You there, Sissy, on your feet and to the center. Yes, now let me see. . . . We need a partner, hmmmm."

Miss Viola's high-heeled shoes clicked back and forth in front of the opposite wall of sweat-soaked chairs.

"Please, God, don't let her stop here." Every week the same silent prayer rose from the line of dumbstruck boys. I imagined reading a cartoon bubble over each head, "I'm really not here. I can't see her, and she can't see me."

Yeah, right again, I thought.

The pacing stopped, soles squeaked as shoes turned, then a staccato *click, click* signaled that Miss Viola had made her selection. She leaned over from her waist and smiled at the partner she had detected behind those pretend curtains of invisibility. From my side of the room the skirt of her dress seemed to slide around and across her vast elasticized rear and down into a waterfall of blue chiffon that puddled just above the toes of her shoes.

"You, Albert," she breathed into the pair of glazed eyes. "Yes, you will be a fine partner to start. Come, come now. Take your position, please."

Albert, whose nickname was String, shambled as slowly as he dared toward me and center court. You always knew String by the way he moved, like a pair of old tennis shoes. There didn't seem to be much more than strings holding him up or together.

Delores and the others giggled behind me. I didn't have to guess why. String was tall and thin; I was short and round, and there wasn't much chance of carrying out Delores's orders now.

"Hey, Sissy."

"Hey, String."

"Quiet, leaders! Now take your positions, please."

From two feet away String reached across center line and placed his sweaty right hand on my waist. My pink organdie turned red. His left arm stretched out, then up in a sharp angle, just like a school crossing guard.

My own slippery hand went up to his right shoulder, and as I stretched to reach for the invisible stop sign he held, we both lost our balance and stumbled—me forward, String back.

"Pleeease, children."

Miss Viola swayed her way over to the phonograph. She held the record gently between her two palms, her breath whooshing across the black surface. Then she put the record in place, settled the diamond needle into the grooves, and the gym filled with scratchy static.

"On the count of three now . . . ready . . . one, two, three, one, two, three." "The Blue Danube" began.

String's muttered counting sent hot puffs of air across the top of my head. I stared directly at his fourth shirt button, yellowed and cracked on one side. My own breathy counting blew the frayed threads up and down. Above them—way above them and a mile of white starched shirt was String's neck and ears. Behind me was Delores and the memory of her threats.

"If you don't do it, Sissy, you're out of the Young Ladies Development Club. Of course, if you aren't grown enough, *Passion's Secrets* magazine is definitely off-limits too, and you won't be allowed to read the rest of *So Now You Are a Young Lady.*"

Delores was obsessed with babies, boys, and sex. We had already read about budding breasts, and we finally figured out babies didn't come from praying, but we still didn't know exactly what part boys had in it all. We spent the entire spring reading everything we could sneak or steal about the subject, but we couldn't find detailed instructions. So Delores paid two dollars to an older girl named Angie just to rent *Passion's Secrets* magazine for tomorrow's club meeting, and the only way I was going to get to read it was to make passion puffs on String Johnson's neck. According to Angie, "You just blow on a boy's neck and ears until he gets these red spots everywhere. That means that he's hot and bothered and you have sexual power. That's the way to get a boy to like you a lot."

Delores paid another fifty cents for that extra piece of information and then made up a new membership rule: "Each member must prove her sexual power, otherwise, she's out."

Some people think being first is lucky, but that's not exactly true. Delores always had someone else test things out before she tried them—just in case there might be a few glitches. So there I stood, facing String's yellow button and wondering if I had enough of that sexual power to get him bothered. He was already hot.

String and I fumbled our way through the first set.

"Children, your steps are too wide. They must be graceful, light, floating, like so!" With that, Miss

Viola twirled herself around the gym floor, dipping and swaying like some rowboat way out in the ocean.

String and I tried again, tilting and stumbling toward Delores's side of the room. As we waltzed in front of the line of chairs, I heard Delores sneer, "Bet she doesn't do it. She's still such a baby, not even budding yet. But she IS my cousin, and well, you know how it is with family. I have to give her a chance."

Some chance, I thought, gazing up at String's earlobes. Little fuzzy hairs grew underneath them and down along the edge of his jaw. Sweat traced dirty paths down the same line. String's mama would have been ashamed, I know. Like mine. I knew String's view was just as bad. Mama always fussed about my crooked part and stringy hair.

We counted our way to the other side of the gym where the row of dumbstruck boys had suddenly come to life with punching elbows and muffled words. Just as we dipped in front of Donald Coates, his leg snaked out between my feet. I stumbled, but String jerked his stop sign up higher, suspending me for a second in midair. "The Blue Danube" came to an end just as my feet hit the floor.

String and I were last in line for punch and cookies. Rose-like spots bloomed red on my chest, under my arms, and at my waist where String's hand had touched it. The collar of his shirt was the only evidence of the starching and ironing his mama had done. The strawberry punch slid cool and easy down our throats. The floor fan drew me to the far corner. Delores and the other girls whispered and giggled. String hunched over the punch bowl, and the other boys pushed and shoved one another like they always did.

"Sissy, you and Albert take the center again."

Miss Viola crisscrossed the gym floor matching boy to girl until she ran out of boys. Delores got paired with Angie.

"Positions, please!"

String's hand drooped a little lower this time, making it easier for me to reach him, but now the sweat had blended with the sweet sticky punch and oozed between our fingers, gluing us to one another. But I didn't have time to worry about it much because the music started and Delores maneuvered Angie toward us, deliberately bumping String and stepping on the back of my heel.

"Do it," she hissed, and dipped away before Miss Viola could catch her.

Across the floor we went, counting and dipping, a kaleidoscope of moving feet, hands, and mouths,

String sweating, Delores twirling, her mouth shaping the words over and over. "Do it. Do it. Do it."

"The Blue Danube" swelled and peaked. String pulled back slightly, his sticky palm sucking at mine, and just as the music paused, there was a loud *thubbbb* as the sweat and sugar glue gave way.

In that half beat of silence, recognition of that sound registered on every face in the room, and I knew my chance had come. I pressed my palm hard against String's, pulling it away quickly time and time again. The sound grew wetter and grosser with each pull. String blushed. I pressed again. He smiled. Faster and faster our palms pulsed back and forth, until finally he could last no longer. The whole length of his upper body doubled over toward me. I gulped for air, cheeks puffed, mouth pinched, and just as his neck bent level with my shoulder, I let it go. A blast of hot air caught String mid-neck and washed up over his jawline and straight into his ear. The hand holding my waist clapped loudly against the wet redness of his ear, the long body lurched away from me, and String fell backward with a befuddled look replacing his wide, loose smile.

Delores and Angie twirled behind him just in time to catch the force of his backward lurch. They stumbled; String reached to grab them while his other palm still stuck stubbornly to mine. The four of us tumbled and one last long *thubbbb* broke the silence of the room.

Miss Viola shrieked and rushed to lift me off the top of the heap. I stood looking down in amazement. Large, red welts blistered the right side of String's neck, face, and ear. Delores's "Wednesday" panties shone like the moon, and Angie was out cold from the fall. Dancing lessons were canceled for the rest of the day.

Later that afternoon Granny brought ice packs to Delores on the front porch. It seemed that when she had fallen, Delores was sandwiched sideways between Angie and String. In the struggle to catch their breaths, both of them had breathed a lot of hot air down Delores's neck, and now passion puffs blossomed beautifully above her budding breasts.

On my way to cancel the Young Ladies Development Club meeting the next day, I passed String on the sidewalk.

"Hey, Sissy."

"Hey, String. Oh, String, I think this is yours."

I tossed the cracked yellow button from his shirt high in the air. He caught it, glanced down, and then leaned toward me like he was going to whisper something in my ear.

Instead of words, a soft, warm puff of air tickled my neck, sending goose bumps all the way down my back. I couldn't help my giggle. String stepped back wearing his lopsided grin, and without saying another word he loped on down the street whistling loudly.

Wow! I thought. This sexual power stuff is somethin' else!

The Gospel Truth About Great Grits

"Elease, if you're thinkin' about goin' to Birmingham, you are liable to get yourself killed, you know?"

"Jus' what do you know so 'bout Birmingham, Sissy?" she answered, sliding the words out slow and staring hard at me.

"I asked you not to call me Sissy anymore; it's a baby name. My name is Amy Claire. And I know a lot about Birmingham. If you would listen sometimes, you would too. The news people are sayin' that colored people that march there are gettin' killed. Seems like grown people ought to have better things to do than march in parades. Why are they marchin' anyway?"

I didn't really expect Elease to answer me. She never talked about that kind of stuff around Granny's house. But she surprised me that day.

"Dey're marchin' 'cause dey's tired, girl—tired of jus' listenin'," she said. "And it ain't no parade. It's a march—a march fer civil rights—a march to get what's right fer folks. Fact is, grown people got nothin' better dat dey should be doin'. It's time— and since when do you listen to de news?"

"I don't, but I heard Granny and Big Daddy talkin' about it the other night. They said you ought to be listenin' to what's going on down there, if you're thinkin' about goin'."

"Humph," she snorted, and then stood for a while not saying anything, just staring out of the window toward the chicken yard. But she didn't stay quiet for very long. She turned around and started fussing at me again. "Listenin', huh? You de one ought to be listenin'—listenin' to me! If you is so grown, you ought to be cookin' and helpin' out some. How you ever goin' to take care of yo'self, huh? Talkin' 'bout baby names and such! When you start actin' grown, I'll be mighty glad to call you Miz A-m-y C-l-a-i-r-e, ya heah me?" Elease drawled out my name in a sassy way. "Now get on over heah and get yo'self to cookin'."

Her words sounded hard. I couldn't figure out exactly what was going on with Elease, but I thought it probably had something to do with those marches. Ever since the preacher told Granny that he had heard that some of the coloreds in town were going down to Alabama, my whole family had been stirred up. Granny cried all the time, and when the subject came up, Big Daddy muttered about "danged fool ideas." We knew that Elease had cousins in Birmingham who were marching for civil rights, but she had never told us that she wanted to do it too. Something was up, though, because she didn't seem happy at all, and she wasn't talking about anything except what I should and shouldn't be doing. She had fussed and grumbled at me every day. I couldn't seem to do anything right.

I thought maybe if I talked to her about it, Elease might just tell me straight out that she wasn't going to go, and then everybody would settle down. It was all Granny and Big Daddy could talk about at night after Elease left. They said she would be in for a lot of trouble if she went down there. Plenty of folks in town wouldn't like it at all, even the preacher. I heard him telling Granny that the colored churches were taking up all kinds of money to send people to march, but they didn't want white folks to know about it. I thought maybe that was why Elease wouldn't take me to church with her anymore. Every time I asked to go with her, she said, "It don't suit this time, Sissy." But it always suited just fine before these last few weeks.

One night Big Daddy said that if Elease went down to Birmingham, she might not be able to come back to live here. Folks won't trust her anymore. Folks will think she's acting uppity, and then they'll make life real hard for her. And Big Daddy said that people will give him a hard time too if Elease starts making problems and he keeps her working here for us.

Granny lost her temper when he said that, and she yelled at him, "Who cares what other people think?"

And Big Daddy said, "We have to care what they think, 'Melia. We've got to live here. It doesn't matter how *we* feel about Elease. It's just the way things are between most whites and coloreds these days."

Granny didn't like that at all because she stood up and yelled back at him, saying, "Well then, I'll ask her about it. Then she won't go. I know she won't." But even if Granny told Elease what people were saying, it wouldn't make Elease talk if she didn't want to. She's a real private kind of person, and besides, I thought maybe she knew about the talk anyway and that was why she had been so quiet these days.

Just thinking about what Big Daddy had said and that Elease might not be able to come back to us if she went to Alabama was like knowing ahead of time that somebody was going to die. Everybody in the family must have felt that way too, but they never did talk to her about it. We just all started trying to cram everything into the little bit of time left. Even Elease was cramming things in—like teaching me to cook. For some reason she had set her mind on doing just that—like cooking was the most important thing in the world. And for days after school I had been up under her in the kitchen, writing down the recipes on note cards that I stacked in the red plastic napkin holder where Granny kept her paper odds and ends and the green stamps she liked to save.

"Ya goin' to lose dose cards like dat, chile. Find somethin' better to keep 'em in."

"I'm not a child, Elease, and I'm not goin' to lose 'em," I snapped back at her, tired of being bossed around. "You know, I should be the one goin' to Birmingham. Colored people aren't the only ones who could use some civil rights around here! I'm tired of havin' to listen to everybody tell me what to do. I'd like to get what is right for me too."

"What you talkin' 'bout, girl? Gracious, Lord have mercy!" she muttered, not giving me time to answer because she went on talking about cooking.

My cooking lessons began with eggs, and then we tried fried chicken, but my first batch turned out raw.

"You jus' hurryin' through, Sissy," Elease fussed.

So I turned down the gas and cooked the next batch longer, just to hush her up. That time the chicken burned and stuck to the bottom of the pan and smoked up the kitchen something awful.

"Payin' no mind," she grumbled as we fed it to the pigs.

But my stack of recipe cards was growing along with Granny's stamps, and even though most of my cooking didn't seem to be getting any better, my vegetables were fine. They cooked down real good, and Elease nodded her head when she tasted them.

"Dese'll do all right, I think. Jus' you remember dat de secret's in de timin' and de seasonin'. Timin' especially. Dat's what's important."

I wrote that on my card, feeling proud. Then Elease spoiled it all by nagging me about cooking grits. I wanted to leave off cooking grits. I wrote down the recipe just like she said it, and I even asked questions to make her think I was interested. Then stalling for more time, I asked her about the marches. I thought if I could get her to talking, she might forget about the grits. It wasn't the cooking I minded so much; it was having to go to the mill to get the corn ground up that I didn't like. That mill is not my favorite place in this world. All that noise in the middle of woods that ought to be quiet seems not to fit together right. It makes me feel all jittery inside, just like I feel at night when Big Daddy and Granny talk about Elease leaving us. So I kept making excuses to put off going, hoping Elease would change her mind about the grits.

"Elease, if you're not goin' to Birmingham to get killed, why do I need to know how to cook anyway? You'll be here to do it. Besides, I've seen you do it all my life. It can't be that hard."

Elease turned to stare at me again. "Seein' ain't de same as doin', and you are talkin' 'bout somethin' you don' know nothin' about." I got the feeling Elease and I were not talking about the same thing. But then she added, "You jus' scared, and bein' scared of somethin' ain't no excuse fer not doin' what needs doin'."

I hadn't ever said a word to her about being scared, but Elease knew things without being told. Telling her I was scared of that millpond wouldn't have changed anything anyway. Once she made up her mind about something, you just had to go along with whatever she told you. I looked around the kitchen, trying to think of something else to say, but Elease leaned down close to me and took my face in her hands, looking me dead in the eye. "Can't jus' choose de parts ya like, Sissy," she whispered.

Elease has a way of confusing me when we talk and that makes me feel like I really am the little girl she thinks I am, and that makes me mad, so before I could stop myself, my mouth blurted out, "I don't know what you are talkin' about, Elease. Why should I be scared of anythin'? You're the one who ought to be scared—talkin' about goin' to Birmingham! So just leave me alone about it. I'll go get the dumb corn ground up. I'll even cook the grits all by myself tomorrow night, so there!"

"Ain't nobody talkin' 'bout Birmingham but you, missy. And ain't you some kind of fine wid yo' sassy talkin'. Jus' you get yo'self on down to dat millpond den, and we'll see who is so big and brave."

She had called my bluff for sure this time, and I didn't have a choice except to take her dare. I slammed the back door on my way out to the storage shed. I didn't like going in there either. It was crammed full of corn and onions and potatoes, and creepy squeaks and scratchings came from the dark corners where I just knew that snakes and mice hid. I propped the door open so it wouldn't close me up in there while I fit the wooden sides onto my little brother's wagon and threw a pile of corn into it to lug down to the mill. When I had the wagon full, I walked past the open kitchen window on my way out of the yard, and I said just loud enough that Elease might hear, "Sometimes you don't make any sense, Elease, talkin' about cookin' and growin' up and bein' scared and goin' to Birmingham, Alabama, all at the same time."

I heard her "humph" and knew she had heard me.

I had never been to the mill without Elease, and I really didn't know what I was scared about, but scared or not, I couldn't back out this time. I think that being scared and not knowing why is just part of being fourteen—things never feel quite right. It's like being dizzy, and the whole world is spinning around and around you, sometimes fast, and then in slow-motion. And one day you feel so happy, it's like your head won't stay put on your body, but the next day your feet come slamming down hard on the ground. What I told Elease was true, I was tired— tired of listening to everybody else tell me what to do and tired of trying to figure out everything in my head. Why couldn't people just leave other people alone?

When I reached the footbridge, I sat for a long time thinking about all of that and about how the noise that breaks up the quiet of the woods around the pond isn't the way it should be either. The far end is calm and smooth, but there by the bridge the black water churns and foams, racing over the spill- way, down onto the gray rocks below. My eyes fol- lowed the sticks and reeds that tumbled with the water onto the pile of rocks jutting out at the bot- tom. But then they got lost in the foam that bubbled up from behind the boulders, and the water got muddy, black and white all mixed together. I knew that if I watched for too long, my head would start spinning and the roaring noise of the falls would fill my ears to make me feel like I was tumbling backward—down, down into that cold water, and hard against those rocks.

But standing up was even more scary. Moss grows slick and green on the boards, and the thought of walking on it made my toes curl under trying to grab hold of something inside of my shoes. Before when I crossed that bridge with Elease, I had crawled along behind her on my hands and knees. She had never seemed scared. She never looked back. She never even looked right or left; she just stretched out her legs in long, sure steps, and on every trip she sang the same songs.

"Elease, why do you sing all the time?" I asked her on one of our trips.

"Singin' makes a change in things," she answered back.

"What do you mean it 'makes a change'?"

"It gets you through things."

"How's that?" I asked.

"We got 'cross dat bridge, didn't we?"

I thought about that—maybe Elease had been scared too. But if she sings every time she gets scared, Elease must be scared all the time because she does a lot of singing. That didn't make a lot of sense to me, but I didn't have time to think about it for very long, because a breeze blew the wet air of the pond across my face, reminding me that I better get moving. Her singing circled around in my head again, and soon it was like she was right in front of me, and I felt brave enough to try a step on the slick, spongy boards.

But I didn't stay on my feet long. My tennis shoes slid across the moss, and before I realized what was happening, my legs shot out into the air. My stomach hit the edge of the bridge when I fell, knocking the breath right out of me. My fingers dug into a crack between two of the boards, and a splinter burned its way up under one of my nails while I hung there over the spillway trying to catch my breath. The boulders below spit the icy foam up to hit my bare skin, and my heart pounded as loud as the falls. I didn't dare look down.

When I finally clawed my way back up onto the bridge, the first thing I did was to make sure my shirt hadn't hiked up over my training bra. Then I checked to make sure the corn was still in the wagon I had pulled along behind me, because I could just hear Elease fussing about spilling all that corn. After that I sat for a long time on those wet boards. I sat there, hugging my knees and gulping down air, trying to slow down my breathing and stop the roaring in my ears. This was what being scared was.

Maybe Elease had been right, I thought. Maybe I wasn't grown yet, and just thinking about it like that to myself made me feel like that little girl everyone called Sissy.

But it made my insides start churning too, and the longer I sat there, the madder I got at Elease. She didn't have any right to dare me to come out here by myself. If I fell off and drowned in that spillway, it would serve her right. "Then you'll be sorry," I said out loud as if she could hear me.

"Can't jus' choose de parts ya like, Sissy," her voice came back to me. I thought maybe she wasn't just talking to me about grits, and for some reason that made me feel guilty. Elease has a way of doing that even when there is no reason. Usually she starts in on how my daddy doesn't like traveling and having to be away from us, or how hard Mama has to work, just so we can all have extra things. I heard this so clear in my head that I looked around, thinking maybe Elease had followed me, but there was no sign of anyone. Then right out of nowhere the words to the song she always sang when we crossed the bridge came back, making the roaring of the water quiet down and the narrow bridge seem wider. Remembering those words, I took a deep breath and began to crawl across the bridge, pulling the wagon behind me, and singing softly, "Nothing Is Impossible."

I told myself it didn't matter how you did something, as long as you did it, and when I was safe on the other bank I ended with a loud "Amen," just like Elease had always done.

I sat for a while, resting in the tall reeds on the other side. Mosquitoes and yellow flies swarmed around me, rising up in dark clouds above my head, then settling to bite and sting my arms and legs. The bugs had never bothered Elease.

"Why don't they bite you?" I had asked her on one of our trips to the mill.

"Blood's too rich fer 'em," she had smiled, and then tossed her head back proudly.

"An' stop dat scratchin'," she had fussed, without even turning her head to see me digging at the bites. Just like knowing things without being told, Elease could see out of the back of her head too. She had warned me about that a long time ago.

"I do listen to you sometimes, Elease," I said out loud to myself as I rose to pull the wagon up the hill ahead, and I knew that if she had been there she would have laughed.

I stopped every now and then to pick up the ears of corn that fell out of the back of the wagon when the wheels stuck in the sand and jammed against the rocks buried there. It took both hands pushing on the handle to move the wagon backward, but then it angled over into the reeds. I jerked hard to make the wheels jump the sandy ruts, but in the end I had to unload the corn to lift the wagon free.

"Two makes work go easy, girl," Elease always said when I fussed about having to help her at home. Then she would sing one of those gospel songs of hers, piling the guilt right on top of me. I felt it again while I reloaded the wagon, and started up the path.

The sound of the stone mill rises up behind the ridge. The sound comes before the seeing—a low groaning that crawls across the water and the land out there. Slick moss creeps halfway up the building and out over the platform built across the front of it, and some of my corn rolled off the back end of the wagon when I started up the ramp. Once, trying to help Elease, I leaned on the corn and pushed the wagon from the rear, but I pushed too hard, and the wheel caught the back of her bare heel.

"Owww, chile," she had grumbled.

"Sorry, Elease."

"Slow down a piece, missy. Ain't no need to hurry so. Dere's plenty o' time."

Remembering that only made me mad at her all over again. Elease is forever talking about time, especially when I want to do something she thinks I shouldn't.

"Dere's plenty o' time fer all dat business when you gets older," she says.

"But I don't think I will ever get old enough to suit you," I mumbled as I struggled up the ramp to the mill store.

"Afternoon, Sissy," Mr. Tidwell cried, thumping the front legs of his chair down onto the platform and pushing his gray hat back up over his forehead. "Needin' some meal today?"

I walked right up in front of him and stood as tall as I could, about to tell him that my name was Amy Claire, but I stopped myself. In my mind Elease was already fussing, "Ain't no chile I'm 'sponsible fer gonna act so rude!"

So I answered with a short "Yes," dropping the "sir" I knew I should have used, and hoping he wouldn't tell on me.

"Well, come on in, and let's see what we can do."

Mr. Tidwell took the wagon handle from me and held the door so I could go in first. He never did that for Elease. He must have thought I was too lit-

tle to do for myself, so I went back outside for a
minute like I was looking for something, and I let
the screen door slam hard behind me, just to get
even.

Inside, the mill house was dark and damp, and
the musty smell of mildew and corn dust filled my
nose, making me breathe faster for air. I stood still,
waiting for the closed-in feeling to pass.

"Somethin' wrong, Sissy?" Mr. Tidwell asked
when he finally noticed me just standing there.

"Uh, no," I answered. "You should—Elease says
you should just take your usual toll." My voice didn't
sound important like I wanted it to sound—it was
small inside the dark walls.

Mr. Tidwell didn't answer me. I thought maybe I
had made him mad about the toll, but everybody
knew he kept a part of what he ground for his pay.
That way he didn't have to plant corn or tend to it
like the rest of us. His cornmeal was just sitting in a
bag on the shelf waiting to be cooked up.

Mr. Tidwell muttered something under his breath
and wheeled the wagon to the side of the room
where he started to take out the ears of corn.

"I can do it, Mr. Tidwell," I said. He had never
helped Elease with it, and I didn't want him to help

me. For a minute he looked as if he was going to argue about it, but finally he turned away and stepped to the other side of the sheller.

I looked down at the small, dark hole before me. There was a loud click, and the engine started up. The noise from deep inside of the hole sent chills down my back. Puffs of corn dust rose like clouds in the dim light to tickle my nose, making me sneeze.

On all those other trips to the mill I watched as Elease placed her palm flat against the bottom of the ear of corn to push it down into the hole, but she had never let me get near it.

"You liable to grind up some fingers in my meal," she had laughed.

Thinking about that made me hold my breath, and I looked over toward Mr. Tidwell, but I sure wasn't going to ask for help. If Elease can do it, then so can I, I thought. So with my hands shaking, I reached for an ear of corn and pressed it down inside the hole. The sheller gave a shudder and grabbed hold of the cob, stripping the kernels from it and sending them rattling down into a big pan. The cob clunked into a bucket on the other side.

"Well, that's one of 'em," I said to myself. My mind held on to the picture of how Elease's hands had looked and moved as she worked, and I heard myself humming one of her songs while I fed the ears to the monster that gulped beneath the floor. Before long there were two pans of kernels ready for grinding.

"And I still have all my fingers, Elease," I sassed her under my breath as Mr. Tidwell led me farther back into the darkness of the mill. But even as I said it, my knees and hands shook. The noise grew louder—a terrible grinding, scraping sound—and underneath it, the slushing of water and that deep, low groaning again. It came from the giant wheel that turned outside to make the stones inside roll together, one on top of the other, turning the kernels of corn into a golden stream of meal that flowed through a funnel and into the stiff white bags that hung below it. Finally, when the stones grew quiet, I loaded the bags into the wagon, and Mr. Tidwell led me back outside into the late afternoon sun.

Usually he offered me a Coca-Cola and talked about Big Daddy and Granny while Elease went around back to where the big wheel turned. But I didn't feel like visiting with Mr. Tidwell that day. I didn't want to go home right away either, because somehow going home where everything was so stirred up seemed about as bad as all the noise at the mill. So I left the wagon by the door and walked around the platform to the back. Once, I had watched Elease from the corner of the store as she stepped right up to that big wheel that spins the water around, and sends it rushing down the creek and out into the pond. She stood with her hands stretched out to catch the drops of water, and her face turned up to heaven. Even with my hands over my ears and the noise of the groaning wheel, I could hear her singing, and this time, even though she wasn't there, I heard her again. "It gets ya through things," she had said, and I stood for a while listening deep in my mind to her song.

"It's gettin' late, Sissy. Best you hurry on home." Mr. Tidwell's words made me jump out of the quiet spell that Elease's memory had made. The thought of darkness in that place sent another chill up my back, and I hurried away, praying to get across the bridge before night came. All along the path, crickets chirped then hushed as I rushed home. The quiet was so loud there, and it made me feel that much more alone. I thought about the times Elease had made that same trip and wondered if she had ever felt that way.

Then I topped the hill, and there below me roared the spillway. In the dusk the bridge looked darker and longer, the rocks below it, sharper and farther down, and as I got closer, my breathing raced again and my heart pounded.

"Maybe she felt sorry about her dare and came to meet me," I whispered hopefully to myself. But Elease wasn't waiting at the bridge, and the longer I stood there alone, the more afraid I got. Finally I rubbed my eyes to clear them and turned to look across the pond. There on the far side the sun was bright orange and red, and as I watched it sink below the black water line, I remembered Elease's whispering, "Quiet now, and you can heah it sizzlin'."

My mind followed those words to another of her songs, and I listened, repeating the line over and over to myself, "Beyond the sunset, a hand will guide me. . . ." Somewhere underneath those words was Elease's voice telling me that it did matter how I did things after all, so with a deep gulp of air I turned back toward the spillway, letting the music lead me, and I crossed that bridge, standing up for the first time.

I couldn't wait to get home. I just knew that Elease was going to be so sorry she had dared me. She was going to have to eat her words this time. I wasn't scared anymore! I was grown, and I didn't need to be bossed around.

"I'm back, Elease," I yelled as I came in the door.

"So I heah," she said as she dried her hands on a dish towel. She didn't even turn to look at me.

"I had a nice visit with Mr. Tidwell," I lied, hoping to get her to talk.

"Put up dose bags now, afore dey get in somethin' wet on dat table," she answered, ignoring my words.

"Do you want to hear about the sunset, Elease? It was real pretty. I think the older I get, the more I like goin' down there to the millpond to watch it sink in the water."

"Humph," was her only answer as she left for the day.

"Don't forget I'm cookin' tomorrow night," I called to her back, but Elease didn't seem to hear me.

"She's just mad 'cause I won her dare," I said to nobody at all. Elease does not like to lose a dare.

When I came in from school the next afternoon, Granny's radio was on. There had been a bombing in Alabama and more people were dead. Elease was standing by the sink, washing Granny's big soup pot. She stood with one hand held under the running water and the other leaning heavy against the edge of the sink. Her eyes were looking hard at something outside the window, but her face was soft, like it was full of sad things, things I didn't understand. I stood there in Granny's kitchen just watching Elease, wondering if she was thinking about going to Birmingham. I wondered too if she was scared. I knew this was one of those times Granny said would make a picture in my mind—a picture that would last a long, long time. But then the water curled up over the edge of the sink down onto the front of Elease's apron.

"Whooa, Lord, what a mess," she grumbled and then noticed I was there.

"I'm ready to cook the grits now, Elease," I smiled.

"Well, you sho' in a hurry, missy. Dey ain't even grits yet. You go wash up and I'll show you what to do."

"But I'm not dirty. Besides, I know what to do; I don't need you to show me anythin'. Just leave me alone and let me get to my cookin'."

"Yo' cookin'?" Elease cackled. "You look like somebody I'm goin' to turn loose in dis kitchen? Go on and get yo'self clean."

Sometimes it just doesn't pay to argue with Elease. When I came back to the kitchen, she was back at the sink filling the big pot with water. Granny's radio was off.

"Pour some of dat meal down in heah, Sissy."

"But it'll make mush!" I argued.

"Thought you said you knew all 'bout cookin' grits."

"Well, I—I thought you had already done this part," was all I could think of to say.

"Jus' you do it now," Elease muttered.

The meal hit the water, and gooey, gray clumps began to float on top.

"Take yo' hands and do 'em jus' like dis." Elease cupped her hands and dipped them down into the water at the far side of the pot. Then she drew them along slowly toward her body and up and out again. Over and over her hands disappeared beneath the cloudy water, and I thought of the giant wheel turning at the mill.

"Now you gots to pour dis off and see what you got." She tipped the pot and carefully drained the water out over the rim until only an inch or so was left to cover the meal that had settled on the bottom.

"Run in some more water, and den start all over again. De meal's gotta be washed good to get grits, ya heah?"

I washed that meal for what seemed like hours. Each time I emptied the pot, Elease told me to do it again. Finally, when I thought I just couldn't move my hands another time, she came to look over my shoulder.

"Dat's 'bout got it, I think. Drain off de last little bit and let's start cookin'."

"I want to do it myself, Elease. Go on out of here. I can do it!" I argued again.

Elease wiped her hands on the apron that hung down the front of her dress. Then taking the newspaper from the table, she started toward the back porch.

"Fine, missy. You do it yo'self. I'll just sit right out here till you yell fer help."

"In a hundred years maybe, Elease!" I smarted back at her.

Then I turned back to the clean grits and the empty kitchen. I reached for Granny's napkin holder and my recipe cards, but they weren't there.

"Elease, what did you do with my recipes?" I yelled out to her.

"Didn't I tell you to put dem recipes somewhere else! Now ya gone and lost 'em."

"I didn't lose 'em, Elease. They're 'round here somewhere. Besides, I told you I already know how to cook grits, and I really don't need them, so you jus' stop your fussin'." Lying was coming too easy for me these days, but that was also Elease's fault, because she always pushed me so hard.

Back in the kitchen I looked again for the cards, but finally gave up, and started with what I remembered—boiling the water, that was the first step. That was easy, and I told myself I would remember the rest, so I got to work.

Before long, steam rose from the pot, sprinkling tiny drops of water across the stove top. It was time to add the salt. I snapped open the white plastic triangle on one side of Granny's shaker and moved my arm in a circle, just like I had seen Elease do a hundred million times, but as soon as I did that, I realized I had opened the wrong side. Streams of salt poured from the wide hole beneath the triangle, and I yanked the shaker away fast, sending a spray of salt across the stove top, onto the counter, and across the floor. I took another pot, bigger than the first, and filled it with fresh water. Then I added some of the salty water from the first pot, threw a pinch of the spilled salt over my shoulder just for luck, and as the water boiled again, I wondered what to do next.

The hall clock chimed, and from the porch I heard the creak of the rocker and Elease's singing. Her song took me back to all the other times she had fixed grits, and I closed my eyes, picturing Elease cooking, trying to remember what she did. I poured the washed grits into the boiling water and gave them a stir, just like she would have done. Then I put the lid on and sat down to wait.

It wasn't long before the water bubbled out from beneath the lid, hissing its way down the sides of the hot pot and onto the stove top. I turned off the burner, but by the time the lid stopped bouncing, the stove was a mess, and the smell of scorched grits hung in the kitchen air. The grits didn't look burned, so I cleaned up a little around the burner and turned it on again, only this time I turned the heat down low.

I couldn't remember exactly how long Elease cooked grits to get them done, so I peeped into the pot every few minutes to see how they looked. But after almost an hour the pot was still full of water.

Maybe it needs more stirring, I thought, dipping my spoon deep into the pot. It stuck on some of the grits that had lumped up on the bottom of the pot, so I grabbed the handle with my other hand and scraped hard at the glob. The grits came loose with a loud slurp, splashing the boiling water onto my hand.

"Yaowwww!" I screamed, and Elease rushed in from the back porch.

"Don' you ever fight a pot of grits like dat again, chile. You gonna have a nasty burn heah fer sho'," she fussed, grabbing the spoon from my hand.

She dragged me over to the sink to run cold water over the blisters that were bubbling up across the back of my hand. The pain stopped when the water rushed over it, but every time Elease tried to dry it off, the burning would start again, and back to the faucet we'd go.

"You jus' stand dere a while now," Elease ordered, and while the water poured down on my burned hand, she hummed low under her breath.

Finally she patted my hand dry and rubbed it all over with a piece of plant she cut from Granny's window pots. The clear sticky juice oozed over the burned skin, cooling it like the water. Then, singing softly under her breath and making her hands softer than I ever knew they could be, she wrapped a piece of cloth over the burn, and patted my head. I don't know which thing made me feel better, the water, the plant, or Elease's pat.

"Now let me help you wid dis grits," she said, turning back toward the stove and the mess I had made.

"No!" I screeched, my voice sounding harder and louder than I meant for it to. "I want to do it myself."

Elease didn't answer me. She looked one more time at the pot on the stove, then back at me, and headed for the porch again. I went back to the stove.

"Must be too much water," I said to myself as I dipped some of the runny grits into another pot. "I wish I could find my recipe."

The grits boiled again, and I turned the heat lower, not wanting to make another mess. "This time it'll work," I said out loud, and through the open window came the words of another gospel song.

I watched the clock as I stirred. When one hand got tired, I used the other one. Elease started on another verse, and my spoon circled the pot in time with her singing. When she reached the "Amen," I tapped my spoon against the pot edge to loosen the grits that stuck to it, just like I had seen her do.

I settled the lid on tight and decided to make biscuits while I waited on the grits. Biscuits I knew by heart. I sifted and kneaded and rolled out the dough, picturing the way Elease's hands had moved. The grits bubbled quietly. But just as I finished cutting the dough into nice round shapes, the lid on the grits pot lifted and a loud *blurp* filled the kitchen. It must be time to add the butter, I thought. But someone had pushed the butter behind everything else in the icebox, so I had to clear the shelf to get to it and then put everything back in again. By the time I got back to the grits, the blurping was coming louder and faster.

I started to halve the stick of butter, then changed my mind and plunked the whole thing down into the center of the grits. I loved to watch Elease do this— the bright yellow melts into the white grits, puddling, then sliding to the edges, turning it all to gold. But my butter didn't look right. It didn't puddle or slide; it only got blurry at the edges.

Maybe I should stir it, I thought. But the more I stirred, the stiffer and slimier the grits got. When the butter finally melted, the pot was full of what looked like a lump of cement wrapped in yellow grease—not like grits at all. I turned off the burner, knowing I'd have to start all over again. But the hall clock chimed six, and for once Elease wouldn't be

able to say that there was plenty of time. Big Daddy
would be coming home any minute and his supper
wouldn't be ready. I had used up the whole afternoon, and all I had to show for it was grits soup and
a greasy brick.

To make things worse, I heard Elease coming
back into the house. There was no way to stop her
from seeing the grits, so I just sat down at the table
with my head on my arms.

"Have mercy, chile! What have you done to dis
kitchen?"

I looked up to see what she was talking about.
Salt, dried grits, flour, and dough made a white path
across the checked floor from the stove, to the
table, to the icebox, and back again.

I put my head back onto the table. "Just don't
start, Elease. You were right, okay? I can't cook, and
I'm not grown. Everything's just a mess!" I tried
hard not to cry.

Elease surprised me when she didn't fuss. I heard
the water running into a pot as she filled it. I heard her
heavy footsteps walking to the stove and the banging
of my two pots as she pushed them aside. Then I
felt her hand sliding up and down my back keeping
time with the song she sang. The clock ticked away.

I kept my head down until she finished her singing. Her "Amen" was so soft, I wasn't sure I had actually heard it.

"Come on now," she said. "It's time to add de salt."

Supper that night was a little late, but thanks to Elease, everything tasted great! The biscuits rose all light and fluffy, and we had fresh butter and jam to go with them. The ham dripped with Elease's prize-winning gravy, and the grits—the pot the pigs didn't get—looked and tasted just right.

"Sissy, this is great grits!"

"You did a fine job, honey."

"The best ever . . ."

I sat straight and tall in my chair, smiling and nodding, acting just like I had done it all by myself. But from the corner of my eye I could see Elease standing by the sink in the kitchen listening to the radio. There was something different about the way she stood there that night—not droopy and tired like she usually was at the end of the day, but erect, with her shoulders back and her head held up high. And I knew that this was another of those times that I would remember. It was as if she was proud about something, like I had been when I crossed the millpond bridge.

I left the table and went to stand by her.

"What you needin' in heah, girl?" she asked me.

"Nothin'," I answered. "I just came to help you."

Elease gave me one of her looks that said, "Well, I ain't believin' my ears," but she didn't say anything. We stood side by side, washing the dishes, and I watched her as she moved. The water was hot with slippery suds, and I almost dropped two plates, but not one dish came close to sliding out of those strong hands of hers. She handled them sure and certain.

"Elease, I want to be just like you when I get grown," I said, surprising myself with the words.

She didn't answer me; she just reached for my hand and then scooped up some of the suds, holding them up toward the light. Tiny stars danced inside all the little bubbles, and I watched the colors sparkle against our hands—hers large and dark, mine small and pale. We stood there, quiet, but there was something sad in her face when she looked down at me. She didn't say anything, but her eyes looked like they were talking, and the feeling inside of my stomach told me that I didn't want to hear whatever it was they were saying. I reached to hug her, but she pushed me away with a gentle shove, so I tried to be happy just listening to her sing.

Early the next morning I found Granny at the kitchen table twisting a Kleenex around and through her fingers.

"What's wrong?" I asked.

"Elease is gone," she sniffed. "She never even said good-bye."

"Gone? What do you mean she's gone?" I asked, already knowing the answer.

"She's gone off to those marches. Gone and left us after all this time."

"Why, Granny?" I asked.

Granny gave me a teary smile and patted my hand. "Never you mind now. I just wish I could have talked to her, made her see what she was up against. I just wish I could have said good-bye," she answered.

Then she reached for a small wooden box in the center of the table. "This was on the back porch this mornin'," she said, handing it to me. "It's for you."

I had seen that box many times in Elease's kitchen. Her husband, Samuel, made it for her the year before he died. The sides were worn smooth from use, and on the front, burned into the wood, were the words "Elease's Recipes." I rubbed my hand over the top and traced the letters with a shaky finger.

"Why do you think this is for me?" I asked.

Granny reached for the box, turning it over to the back side. There, burned into the wood just as carefully as the name on the front, was my name— Amy Claire.

I sat down at the table staring at the letters of my name on the outside of the box—Amy Claire. It looked so grown-up. But inside, inside of me, I felt like Sissy. Inside I wanted to cry. I wanted to cry because Elease was gone, because she didn't say good-bye, because she hadn't loved us enough to stay.

Then the years played over and over in my mind. I thought of the times she had helped me out—not just with the grits, but all those other times as far back as I could remember. I thought about my trip to the mill and how, not even being there, she had still helped me. I thought about the way Mr. Tidwell had acted, about what the preacher and Big Daddy had said, and then I thought about those marches in Birmingham. In my mind I could see Elease's eyes talking to me there by the sink, and I knew what those eyes had been telling me. She had known what she was up against, and she had said good-bye the only way she could. It was just that none of us had wanted to hear it.

I began to sort through the recipes inside of the box. I came last to the one for grits. I studied it, remembering, then turned it over and began writing on the back.

"What are you doin', Sissy?" Granny asked, looking over my shoulder.

"I'm rewritin' Elease's grits recipe."

"But this is just a list of old gospel songs," she said.

"Yep, that's how I make grits." I smiled, looking deep into Granny's eyes.

"'Precious Memories,'" she read out loud, and I knew she understood when she squeezed my shoulder and sniffed again into her tissue.

I replaced all of the cards and took a deep breath as I traced the letters of my name once more. Amy Claire. My fingers weren't shaking anymore, but inside my feelings were racing and churning like that water at the spillway. I was sad that Elease was gone, but somehow I knew that she'd come back to Midville, and I was glad about that. But then the glad and the sad got all mixed up together. She'd come home all right, but not to us. She'd have her civil rights, and I would be a grown-up Amy Claire. We'd both make grits again, for sure. But it wouldn't be the same. Nothing would ever be the same.

After a while I put my recipe box carefully on the shelf above Granny's stove and started through the door.

"Where're you goin', Sissy?" Granny asked.

"I'm goin' down to the millpond for a while," I said, tossing back my hair and taking a step backward out of the door. I hoped Granny would notice how grown-up I sounded and that I wasn't afraid to go alone. But my shoe caught on the doorjamb and before I could catch myself, I tumbled flat on my back onto the porch. When I caught my breath, Granny was tugging my shirt down over my bra and pulling on my arms, trying to lift me up. She brushed at the back of my shirt and pants and then started laughing out loud.

"What's so funny?" I asked, embarrassed by my fall.

Granny pulled at the seat of my pants, and I felt a cool draft of air rising to my waist. My back seam had split all the way up.

"Maybe instead of cookin', Elease should have taught you walkin', Sissy," she chuckled, sounding just like Elease.

I pulled away from her and stalked up the hall to change my clothes, muttering to myself. Now that I had finally convinced Elease that I was grown, I was going to have to start all over with Granny. So just like I had done with Elease, I turned and shouted, "Don't call me Sissy! My name is Amy Claire!!!"

$15.99

DATE			